WANTED LUCKY LUKE

SCRIPT, ARTWORK AND COLOURS
MATTHIEU BONHOMME

9th CINEBOOK
The 9th Art Publisher

For their careful and exacting proofreading,
my thanks go to Pauline Mermet and Stéphane Oiry.

Matthieu Bonhomme

Original title: Wanted Lucky Luke
Original edition: © Lucky Comics 2021 by Bonhomme
© Lucky Comics
www.lucky-luke.com
English translation: © 2021 Cinebook Ltd
Translator: Jerome Saincantin
Editor: Erica Olson Jeffrey
Lettering and text layout: Design Amorandi
Printed in Spain by EGEDSA
This edition first published in Great Britain in 2022 by
Cinebook Ltd
56 Beech Avenue
Canterbury, Kent
CT4 7TA
www.cinebook.com
A CIP catalogue record for this book
is available from the British Library
ISBN 978-1-80044-044-9

CINEBOOK
The 9th Art Publisher

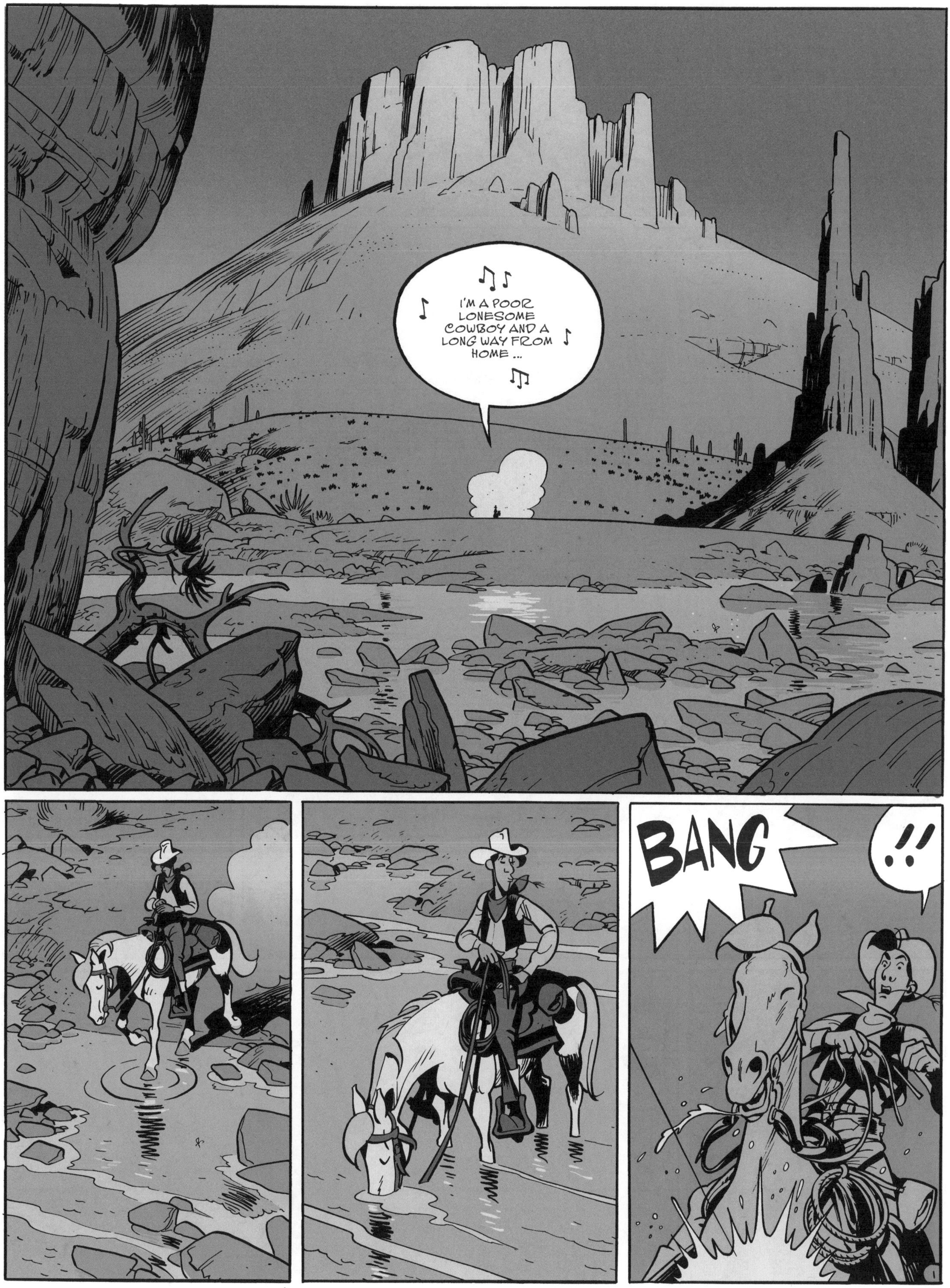
I'M A POOR LONESOME COWBOY AND A LONG WAY FROM HOME ...
BANG
!!

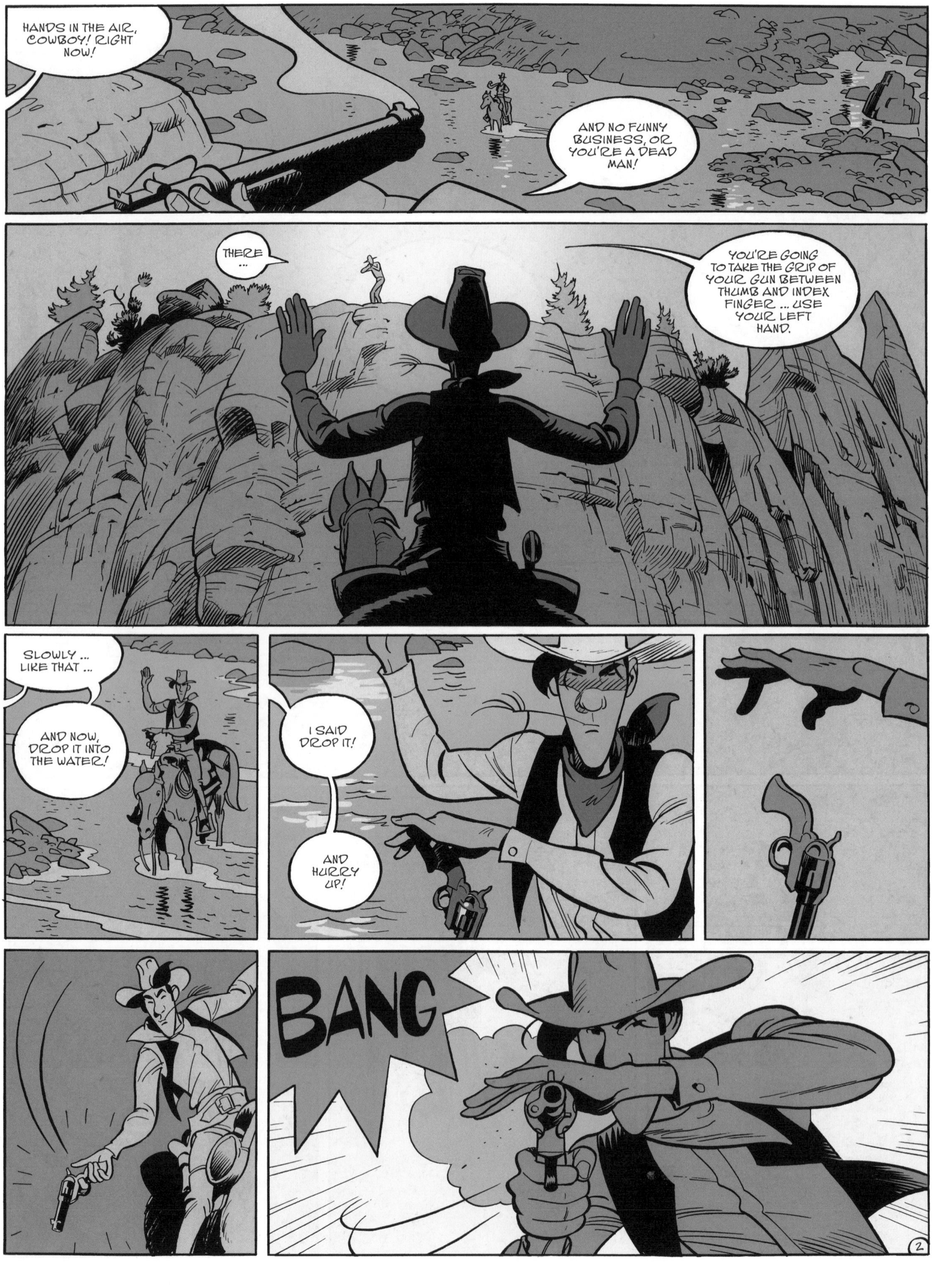
HANDS IN THE AIR, COWBOY! RIGHT NOW!
AND NO FUNNY BUSINESS, OR YOU'RE A DEAD MAN!
THERE ...
YOU'RE GOING TO TAKE THE GRIP OF YOUR GUN BETWEEN THUMB AND INDEX FINGER ... USE YOUR LEFT HAND.
SLOWLY ... LIKE THAT ...
AND NOW, DROP IT INTO THE WATER!
I SAID DROP IT!
AND HURRY UP!
BANG
2

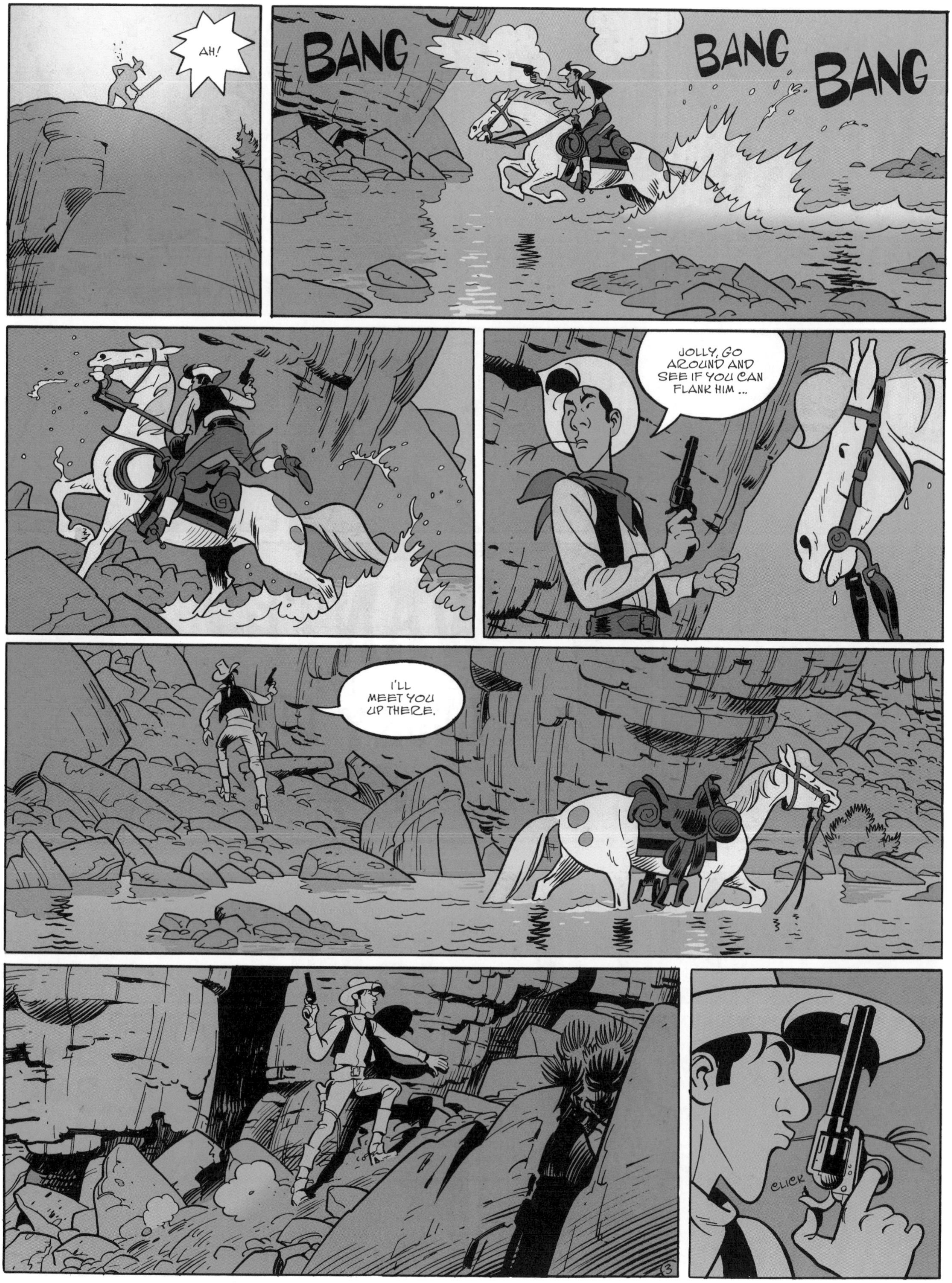
AH!
BANG
BANG
BANG
JOLLY, GO AROUND AND SEE IF YOU CAN FLANK HIM ...
I'LL MEET YOU UP THERE.
CLICK

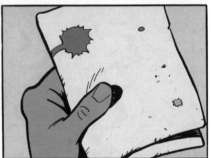

WANTED
ALIVE
LUCKY LUKE
$5,000

BANG
BANG

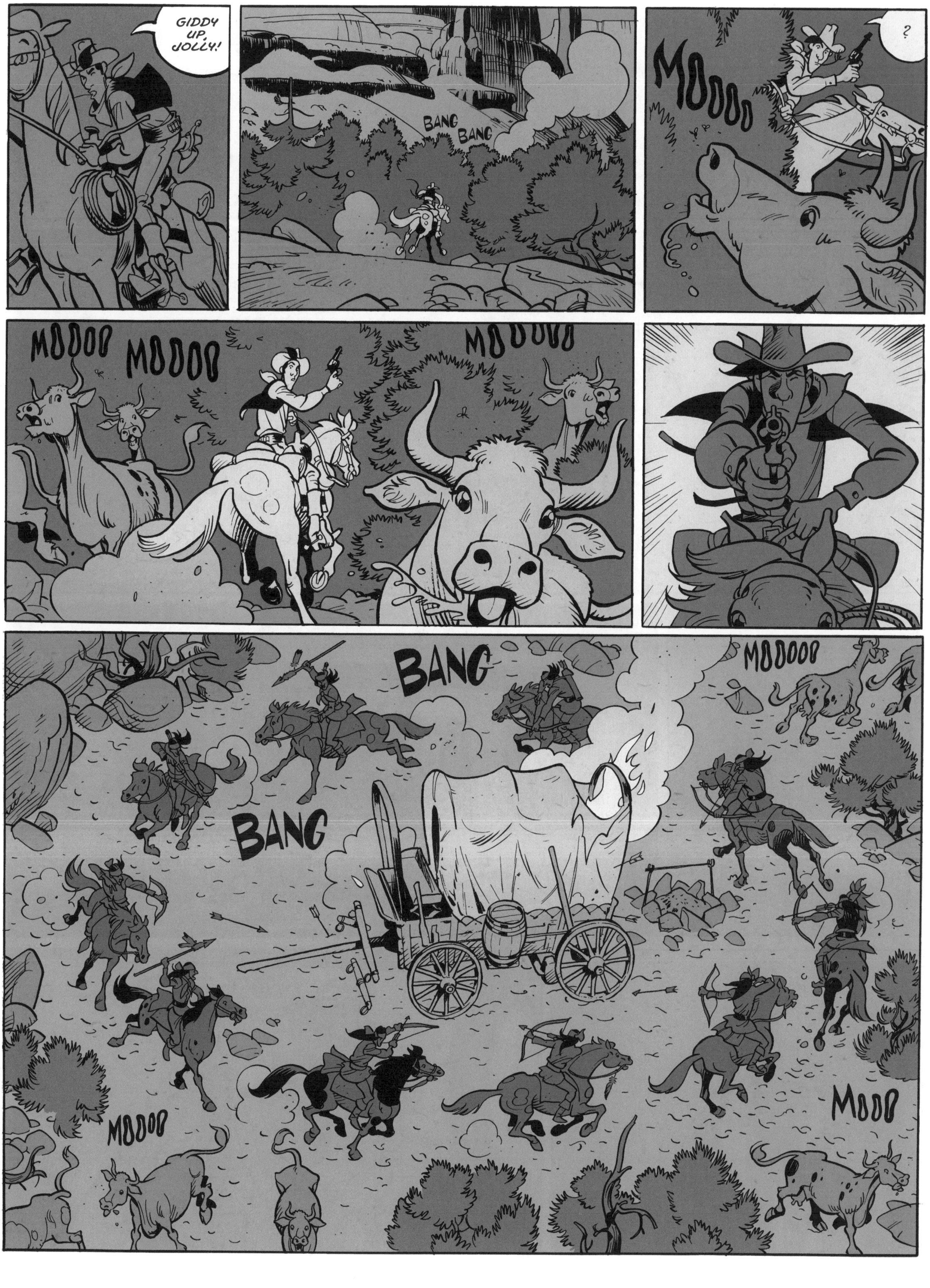
GIDDY UP, JOLLY!
BANG
BANG
MOOOOO
?
MOOOO
MOOOO
MOOOOOO
BANG
MOOOOO
BANG
MOOOO
MOOOO

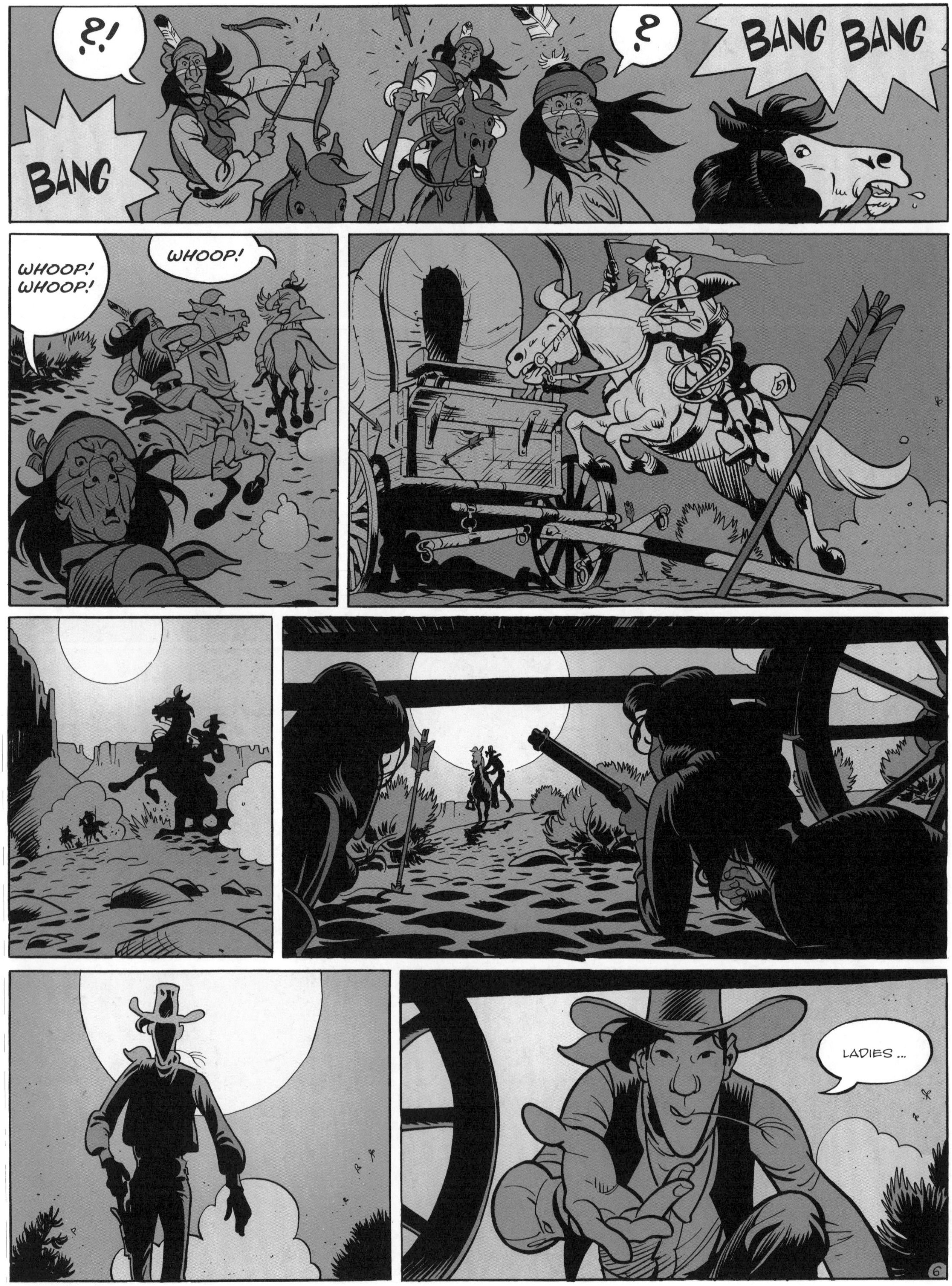
?!
BANG
?
BANG BANG
WHOOP! WHOOP!
WHOOP!
LADIES ...
6

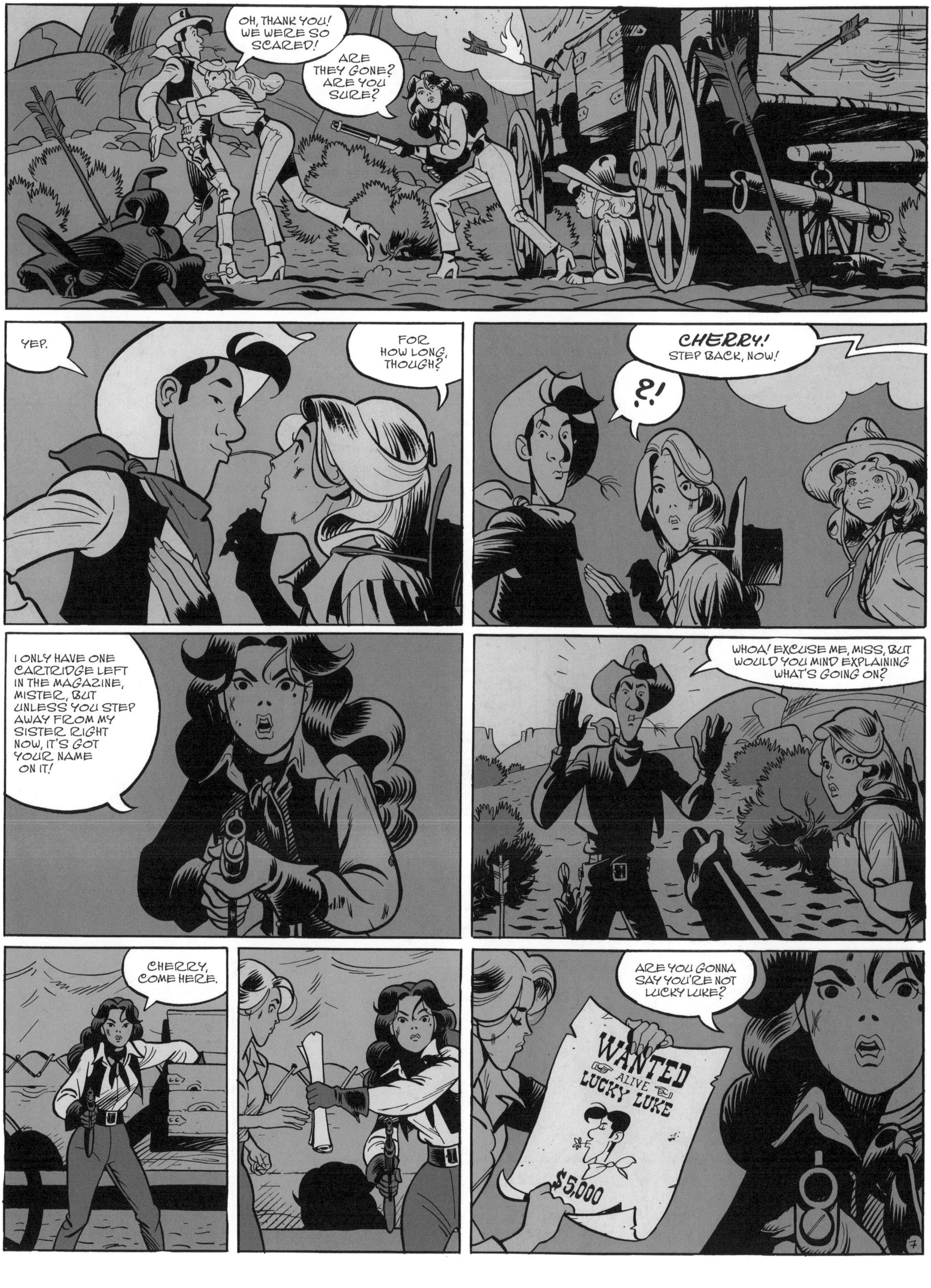
OH, THANK YOU! WE WERE SO SCARED!
ARE THEY GONE? ARE YOU SURE?
YEP.
FOR HOW LONG, THOUGH?
CHERRY! STEP BACK, NOW!
?!
I ONLY HAVE ONE CARTRIDGE LEFT IN THE MAGAZINE, MISTER, BUT UNLESS YOU STEP AWAY FROM MY SISTER RIGHT NOW, IT'S GOT YOUR NAME ON IT!
WHOA! EXCUSE ME, MISS, BUT WOULD YOU MIND EXPLAINING WHAT'S GOING ON?
CHERRY, COME HERE.
ARE YOU GONNA SAY YOU'RE NOT LUCKY LUKE?
WANTED
ALIVE
LUCKY LUKE
$5,000
7

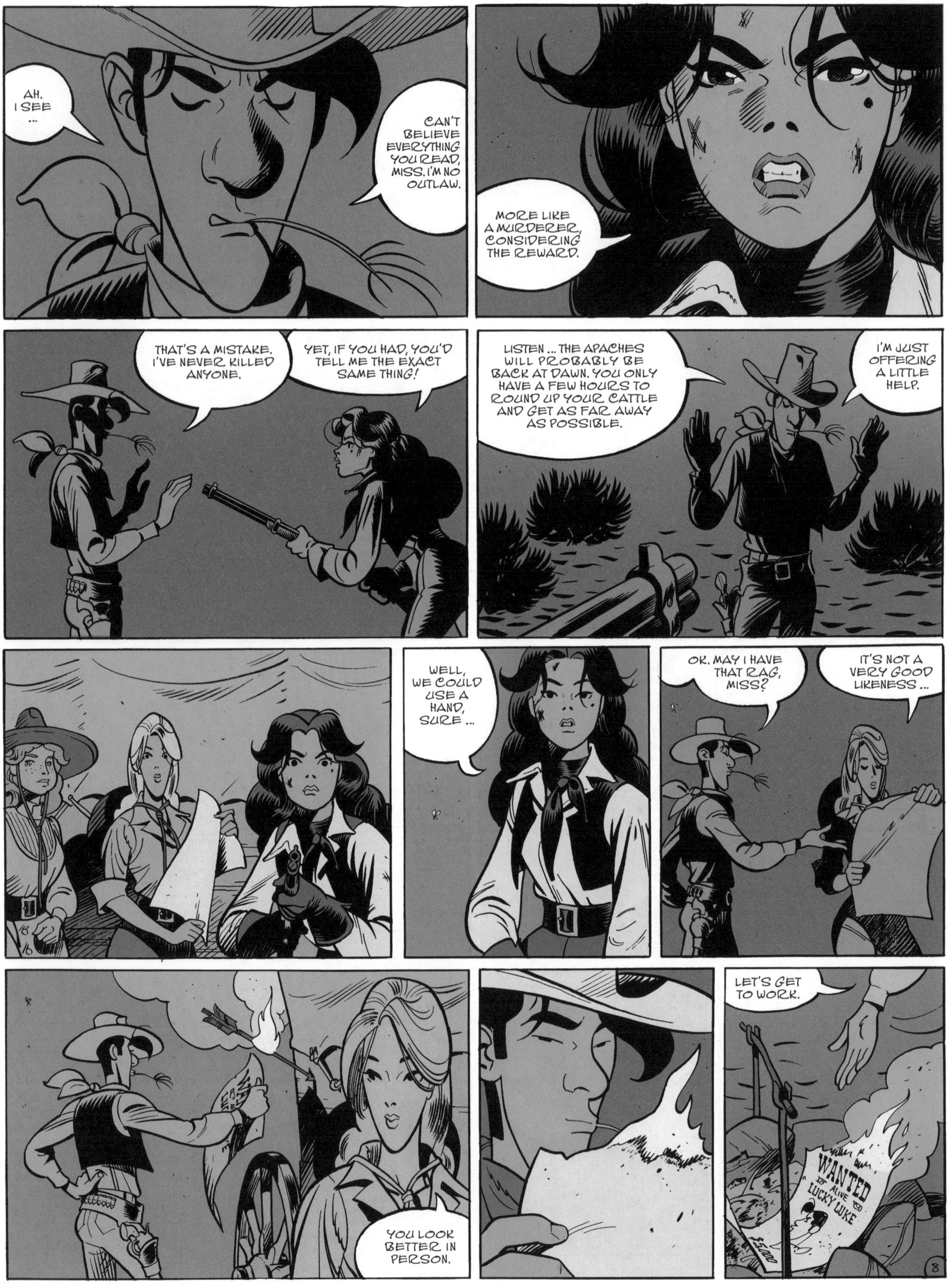
AH. I SEE ...
CAN'T BELIEVE EVERYTHING YOU READ, MISS. I'M NO OUTLAW.
MORE LIKE A MURDERER, CONSIDERING THE REWARD.
THAT'S A MISTAKE. I'VE NEVER KILLED ANYONE.
YET, IF YOU HAD, YOU'D TELL ME THE EXACT SAME THING!
LISTEN ... THE APACHES WILL PROBABLY BE BACK AT DAWN. YOU ONLY HAVE A FEW HOURS TO ROUND UP YOUR CATTLE AND GET AS FAR AWAY AS POSSIBLE.
I'M JUST OFFERING A LITTLE HELP.
WELL, WE COULD USE A HAND, SURE ...
OK. MAY I HAVE THAT RAG, MISS?
IT'S NOT A VERY GOOD LIKENESS ...
YOU LOOK BETTER IN PERSON.
LET'S GET TO WORK.
WANTED
ALIVE
LUCKY LUKE
8

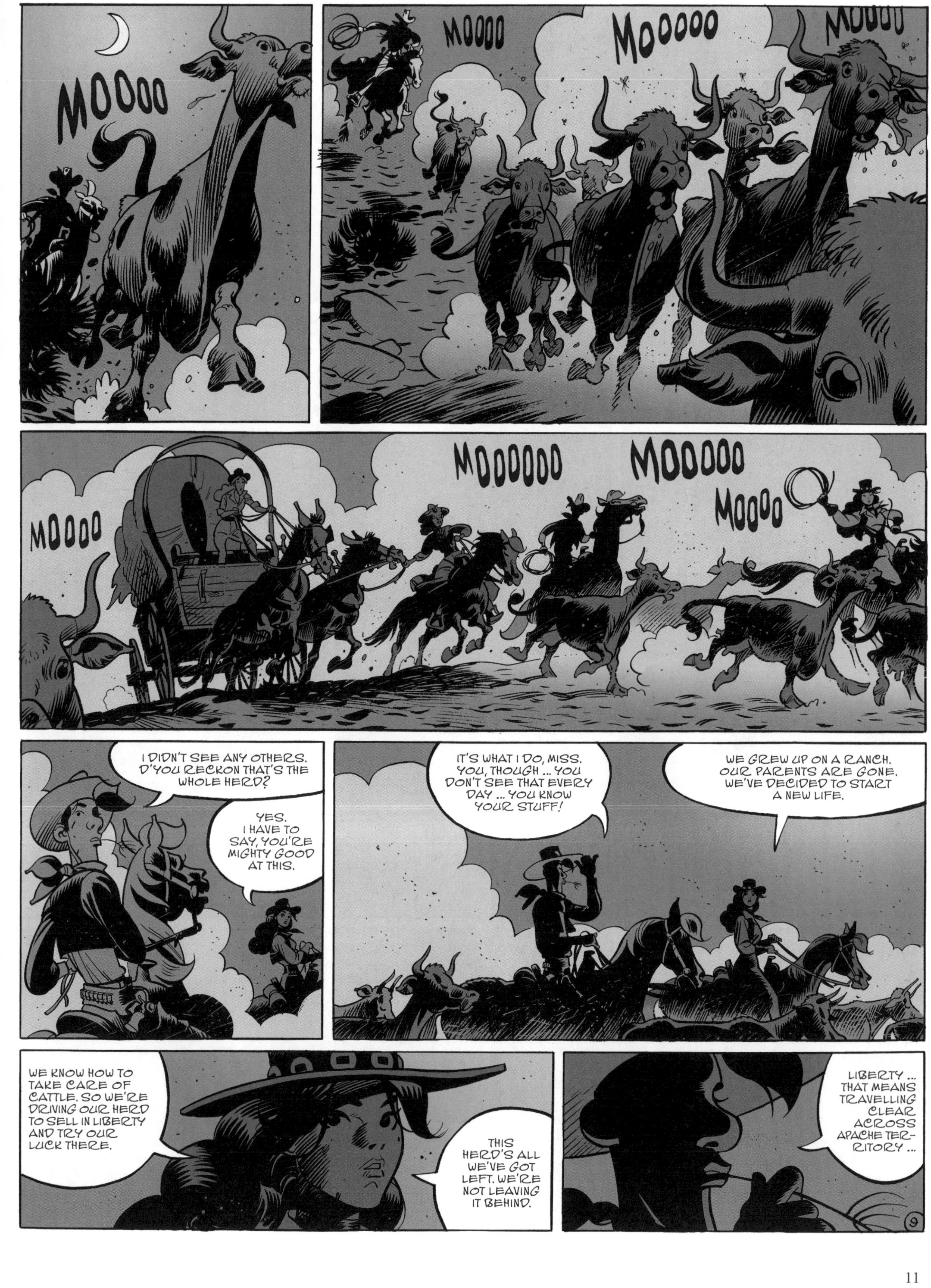
MOOOO
MOOOO
MOOOOO
MOOOO
MOOOOOO
MOOOOO
MOOOO
I DIDN'T SEE ANY OTHERS. D'YOU RECKON THAT'S THE WHOLE HERD?
YES. I HAVE TO SAY, YOU'RE MIGHTY GOOD AT THIS.
IT'S WHAT I DO, MISS. YOU, THOUGH ... YOU DON'T SEE THAT EVERY DAY ... YOU KNOW YOUR STUFF!
WE GREW UP ON A RANCH. OUR PARENTS ARE GONE. WE'VE DECIDED TO START A NEW LIFE.
WE KNOW HOW TO TAKE CARE OF CATTLE. SO WE'RE DRIVING OUR HERD TO SELL IN LIBERTY AND TRY OUR LUCK THERE.
THIS HERD'S ALL WE'VE GOT LEFT. WE'RE NOT LEAVING IT BEHIND.
LIBERTY ... THAT MEANS TRAVELLING CLEAR ACROSS APACHE TER-RITORY ...
9

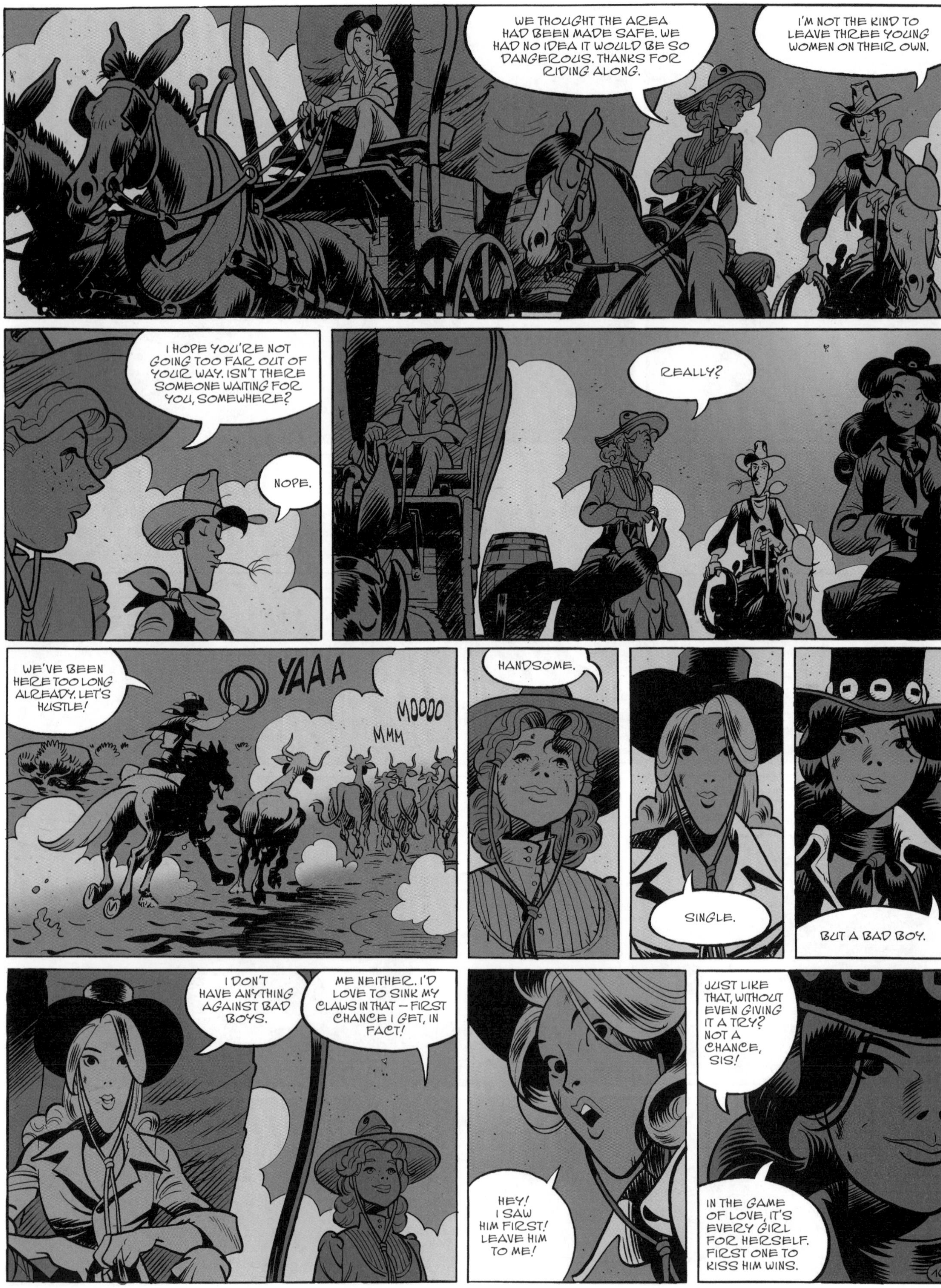

WE THOUGHT THE AREA HAD BEEN MADE SAFE. WE HAD NO IDEA IT WOULD BE SO DANGEROUS. THANKS FOR RIDING ALONG.
I'M NOT THE KIND TO LEAVE THREE YOUNG WOMEN ON THEIR OWN.
I HOPE YOU'RE NOT GOING TOO FAR OUT OF YOUR WAY. ISN'T THERE SOMEONE WAITING FOR YOU, SOMEWHERE?
NOPE.
REALLY?
WE'VE BEEN HERE TOO LONG ALREADY. LET'S HUSTLE!
YAAA
MOOOO
MMM
HANDSOME.
SINGLE.
BUT A BAD BOY.
I DON'T HAVE ANYTHING AGAINST BAD BOYS.
ME NEITHER. I'D LOVE TO SINK MY CLAWS IN THAT – FIRST CHANCE I GET, IN FACT!
HEY! I SAW HIM FIRST! LEAVE HIM TO ME!
JUST LIKE THAT, WITHOUT EVEN GIVING IT A TRY? NOT A CHANCE, SIS!
IN THE GAME OF LOVE, IT'S EVERY GIRL FOR HERSELF. FIRST ONE TO KISS HIM WINS.
10

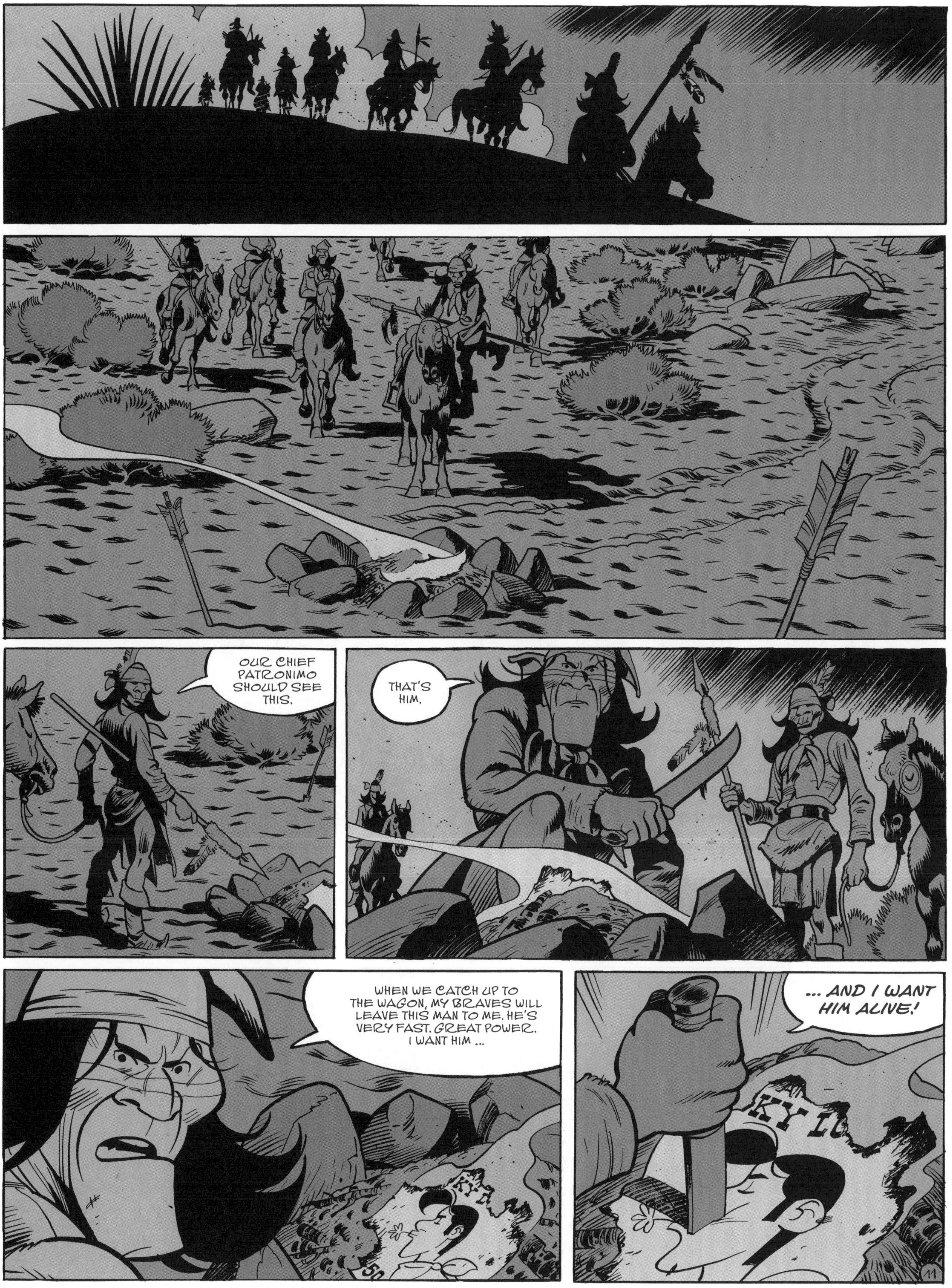
OUR CHIEF PATRONIMO SHOULD SEE THIS.
THAT'S HIM.
WHEN WE CATCH UP TO THE WAGON, MY BRAVES WILL LEAVE THIS MAN TO ME. HE'S VERY FAST. GREAT POWER. I WANT HIM ...
... AND I WANT HIM ALIVE!
11

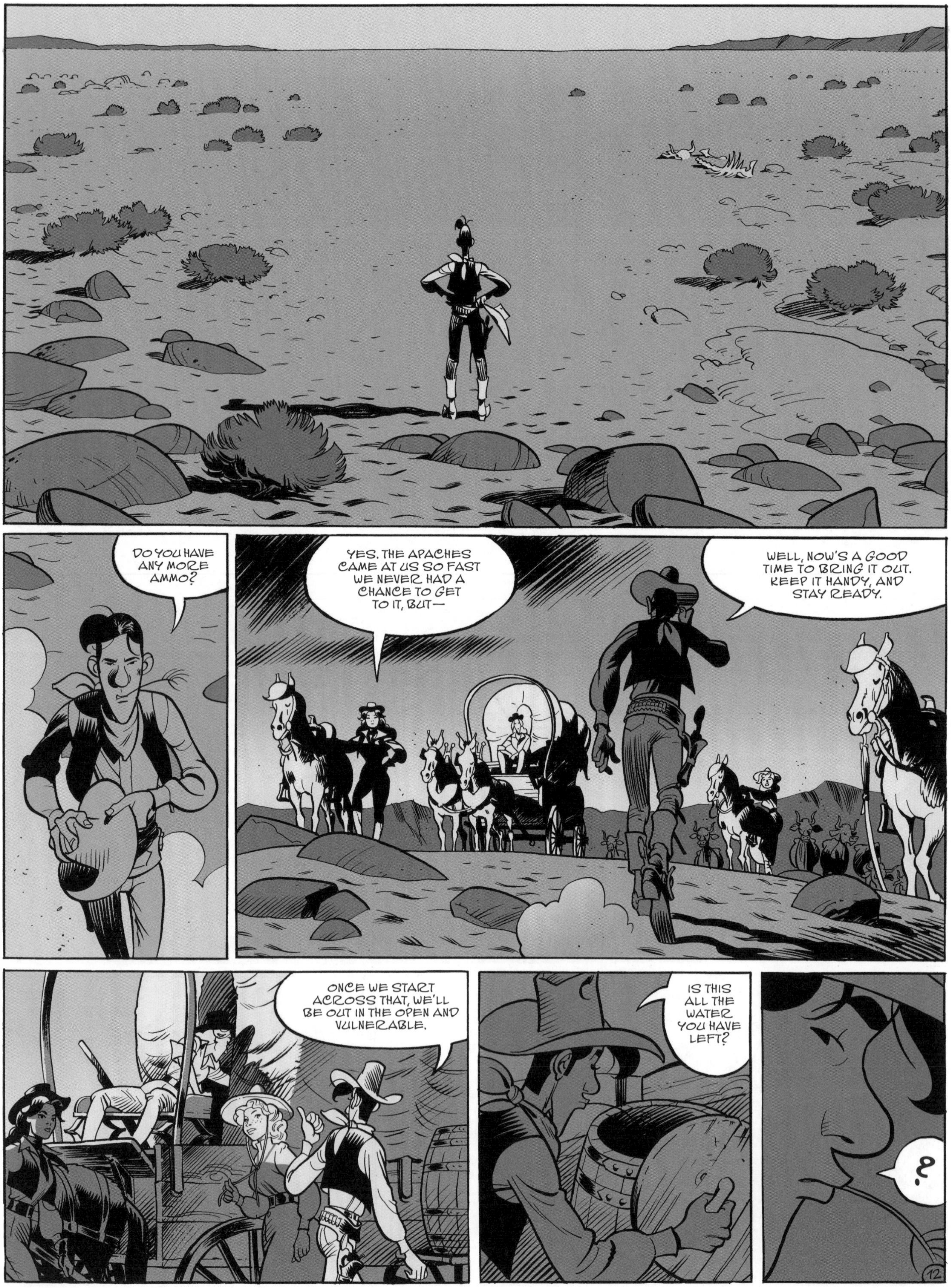
DO YOU HAVE ANY MORE AMMO?
YES. THE APACHES CAME AT US SO FAST WE NEVER HAD A CHANCE TO GET TO IT, BUT—
WELL, NOW'S A GOOD TIME TO BRING IT OUT. KEEP IT HANDY, AND STAY READY.
ONCE WE START ACROSS THAT, WE'LL BE OUT IN THE OPEN AND VULNERABLE.
IS THIS ALL THE WATER YOU HAVE LEFT?
?
12

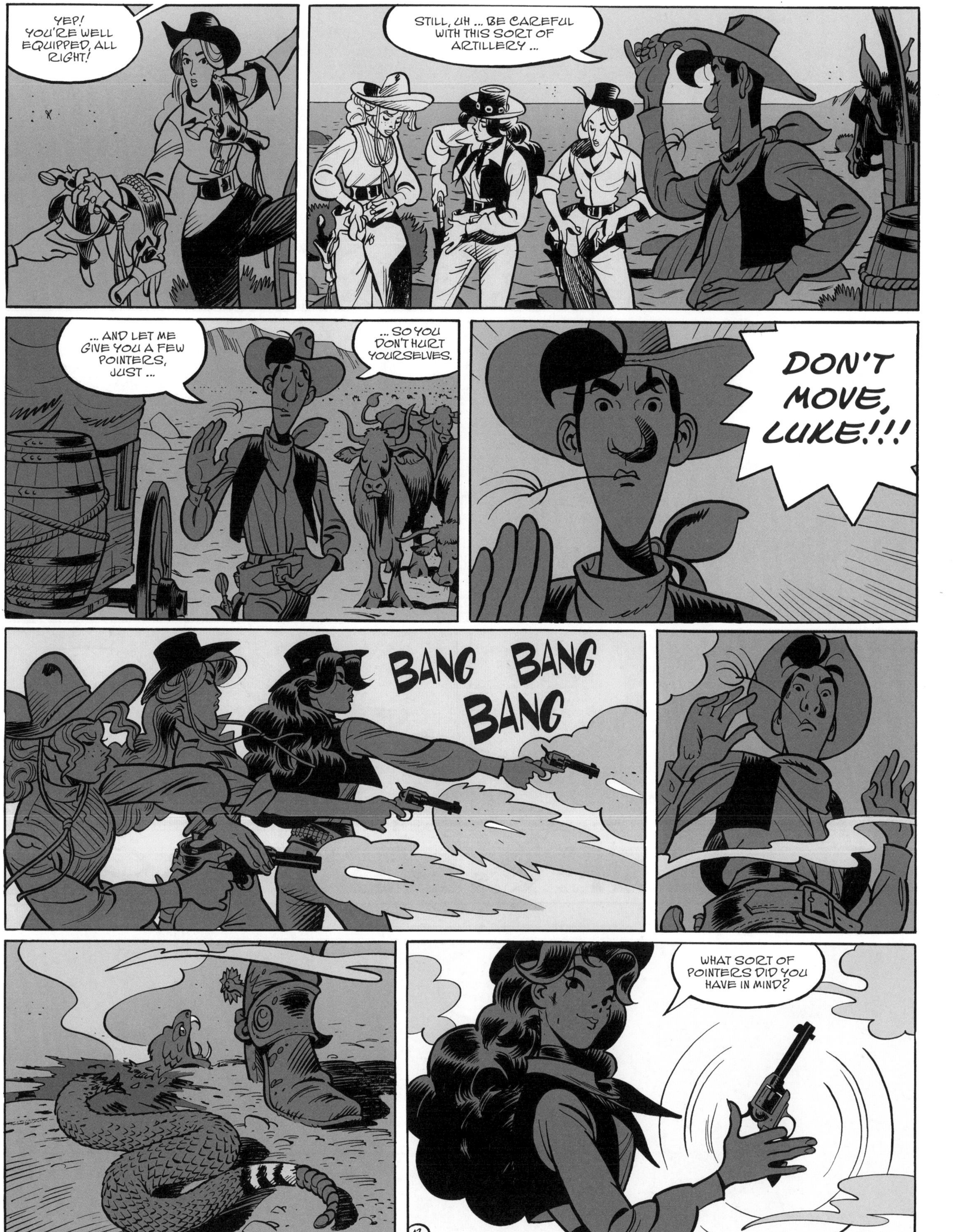

YEP! YOU'RE WELL EQUIPPED, ALL RIGHT!
STILL, UH ... BE CAREFUL WITH THIS SORT OF ARTILLERY ...
... AND LET ME GIVE YOU A FEW POINTERS, JUST ...
... SO YOU DON'T HURT YOURSELVES.
DON'T MOVE, LUKE!!!
BANG BANG BANG
WHAT SORT OF POINTERS DID YOU HAVE IN MIND?
13

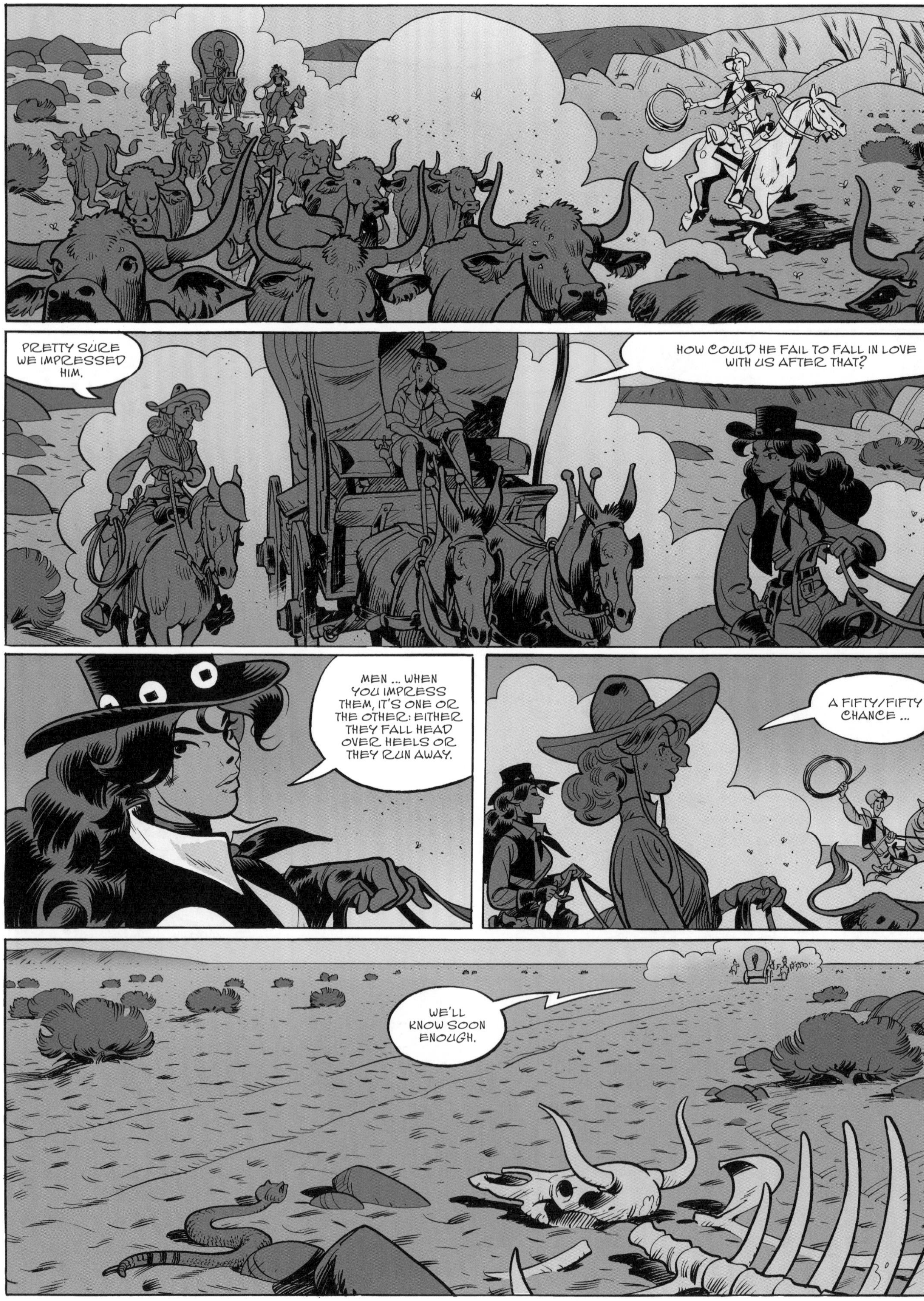
PRETTY SURE WE IMPRESSED HIM.
HOW COULD HE FAIL TO FALL IN LOVE WITH US AFTER THAT?
MEN ... WHEN YOU IMPRESS THEM, IT'S ONE OR THE OTHER: EITHER THEY FALL HEAD OVER HEELS OR THEY RUN AWAY.
A FIFTY/FIFTY CHANCE ...
WE'LL KNOW SOON ENOUGH.
14

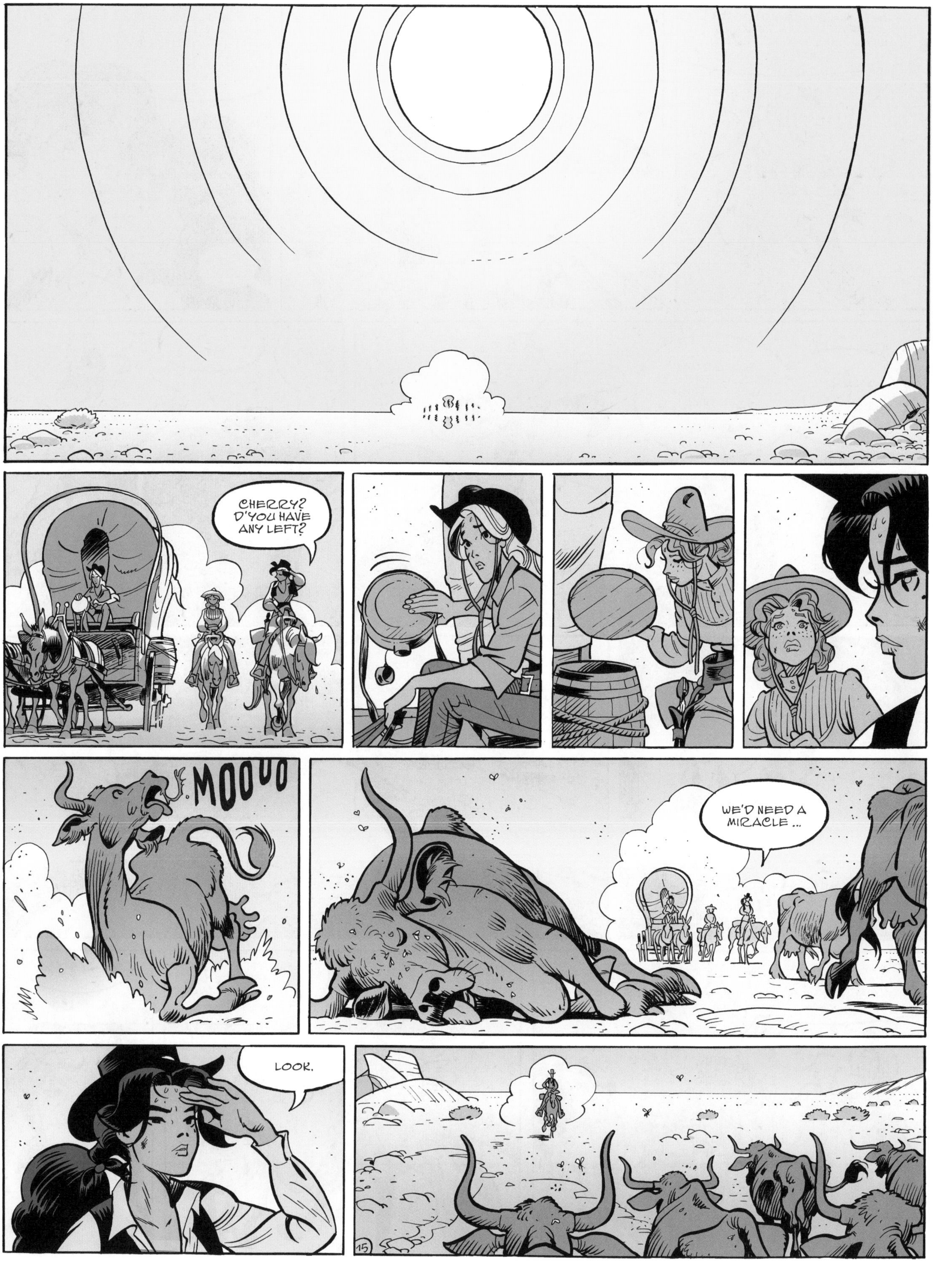
CHERRY? D'YOU HAVE ANY LEFT?
MOOOO
WE'D NEED A MIRACLE ...
LOOK.

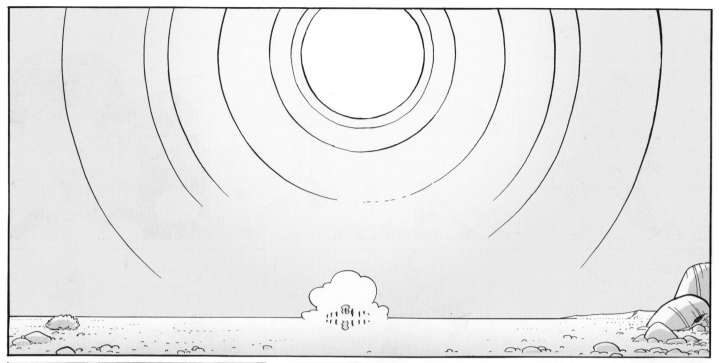

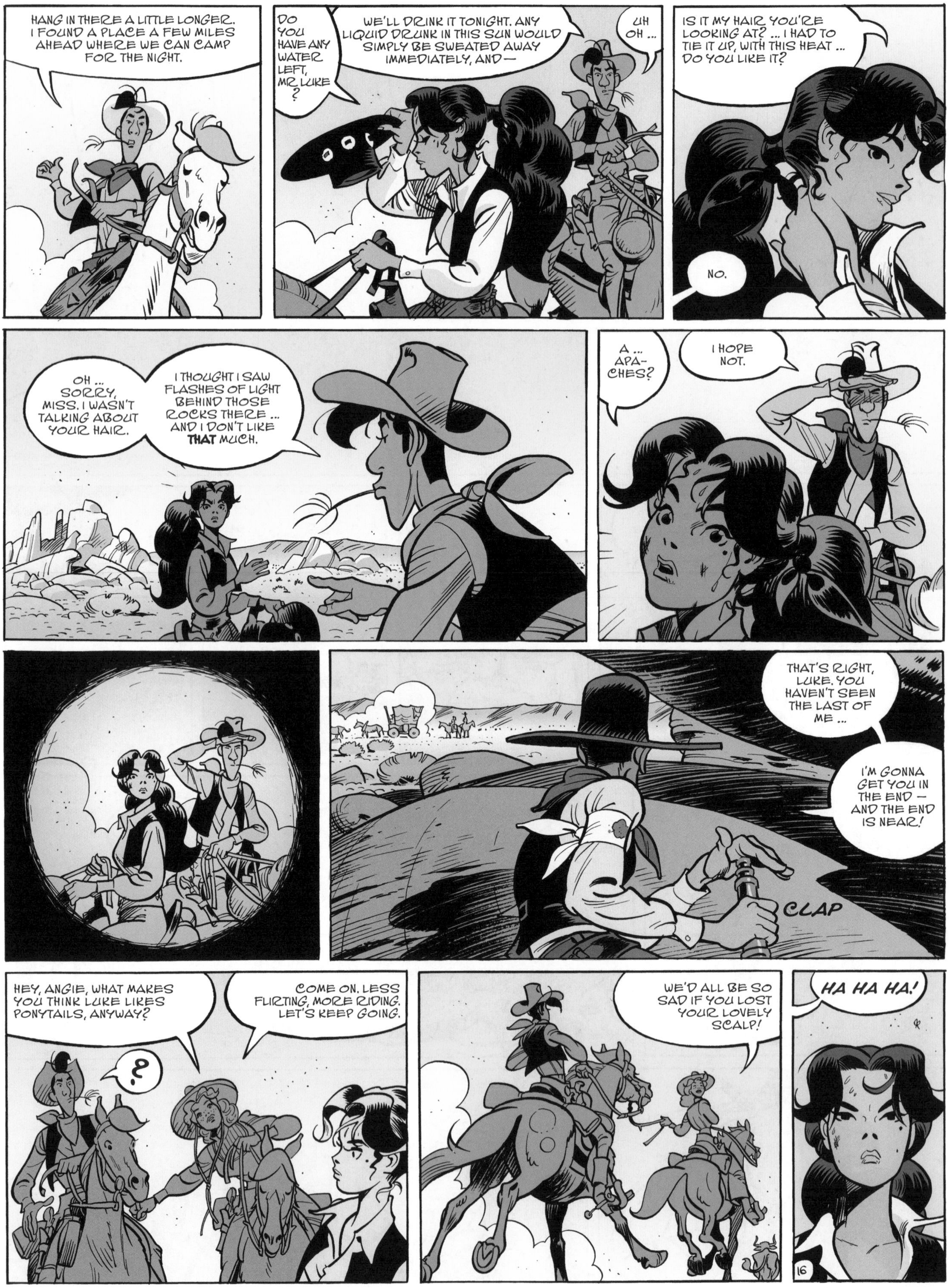
HANG IN THERE A LITTLE LONGER. I FOUND A PLACE A FEW MILES AHEAD WHERE WE CAN CAMP FOR THE NIGHT.
DO YOU HAVE ANY WATER LEFT, MR LUKE ?
WE'LL DRINK IT TONIGHT. ANY LIQUID DRUNK IN THIS SUN WOULD SIMPLY BE SWEATED AWAY IMMEDIATELY, AND—
UH OH ...
IS IT MY HAIR YOU'RE LOOKING AT? ... I HAD TO TIE IT UP, WITH THIS HEAT ... DO YOU LIKE IT?
NO.
OH ... SORRY, MISS. I WASN'T TALKING ABOUT YOUR HAIR.
I THOUGHT I SAW FLASHES OF LIGHT BEHIND THOSE ROCKS THERE ... AND I DON'T LIKE THAT MUCH.
A ... APA-CHES?
I HOPE NOT.
THAT'S RIGHT, LUKE. YOU HAVEN'T SEEN THE LAST OF ME ...
I'M GONNA GET YOU IN THE END — AND THE END IS NEAR!
CLAP
HEY, ANGIE, WHAT MAKES YOU THINK LUKE LIKES PONYTAILS, ANYWAY?
?
COME ON. LESS FLIRTING, MORE RIDING. LET'S KEEP GOING.
WE'D ALL BE SO SAD IF YOU LOST YOUR LOVELY SCALP!
HA HA HA!
16

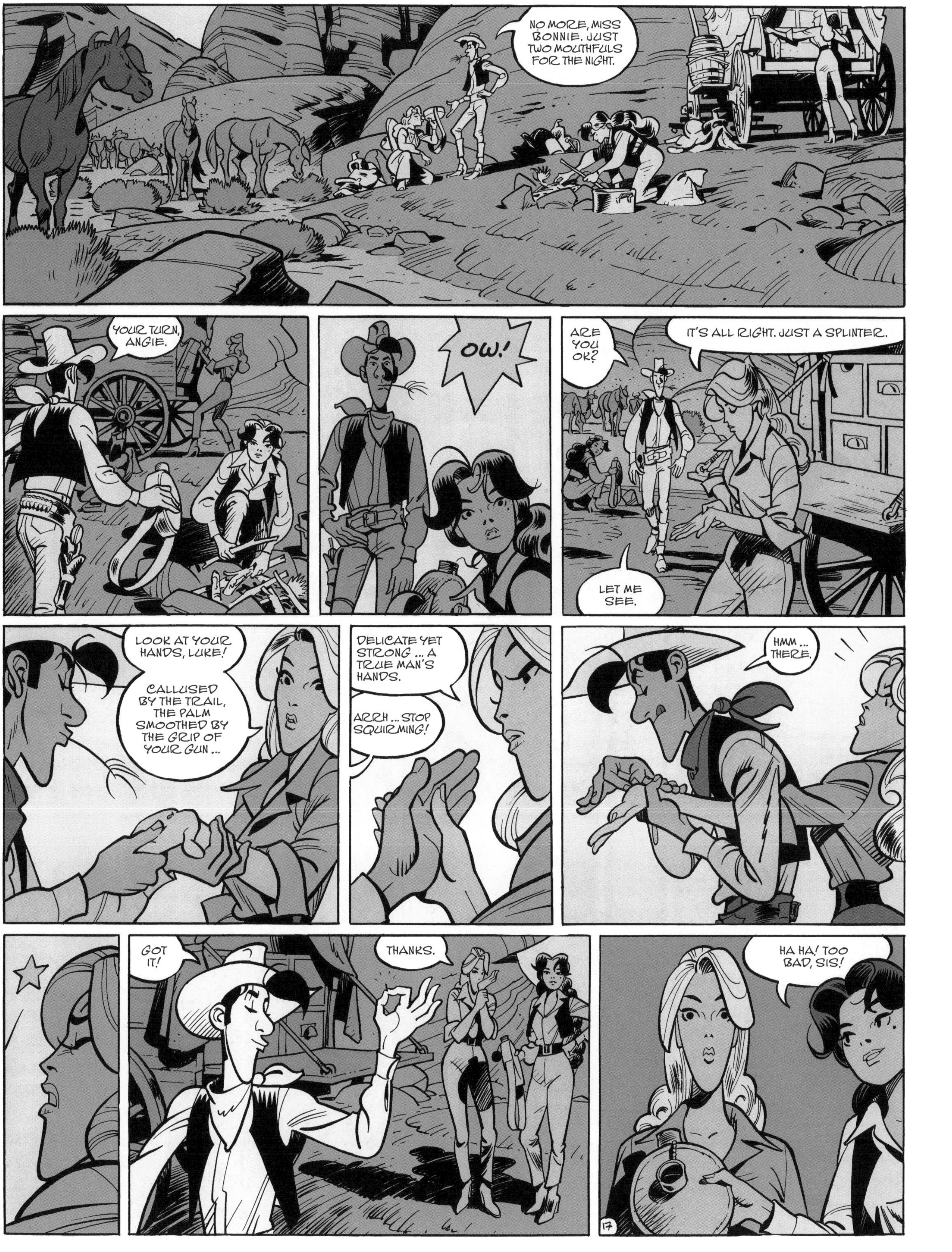
NO MORE, MISS BONNIE. JUST TWO MOUTHFULS FOR THE NIGHT.
YOUR TURN, ANGIE.
OW!
ARE YOU OK?
IT'S ALL RIGHT. JUST A SPLINTER.
LET ME SEE.
LOOK AT YOUR HANDS, LUKE!
CALLUSED BY THE TRAIL, THE PALM SMOOTHED BY THE GRIP OF YOUR GUN ...
DELICATE YET STRONG ... A TRUE MAN'S HANDS.
ARRH ... STOP SQUIRMING!
HMM ... THERE.
GOT IT!
THANKS.
HA HA! TOO BAD, SIS!
17

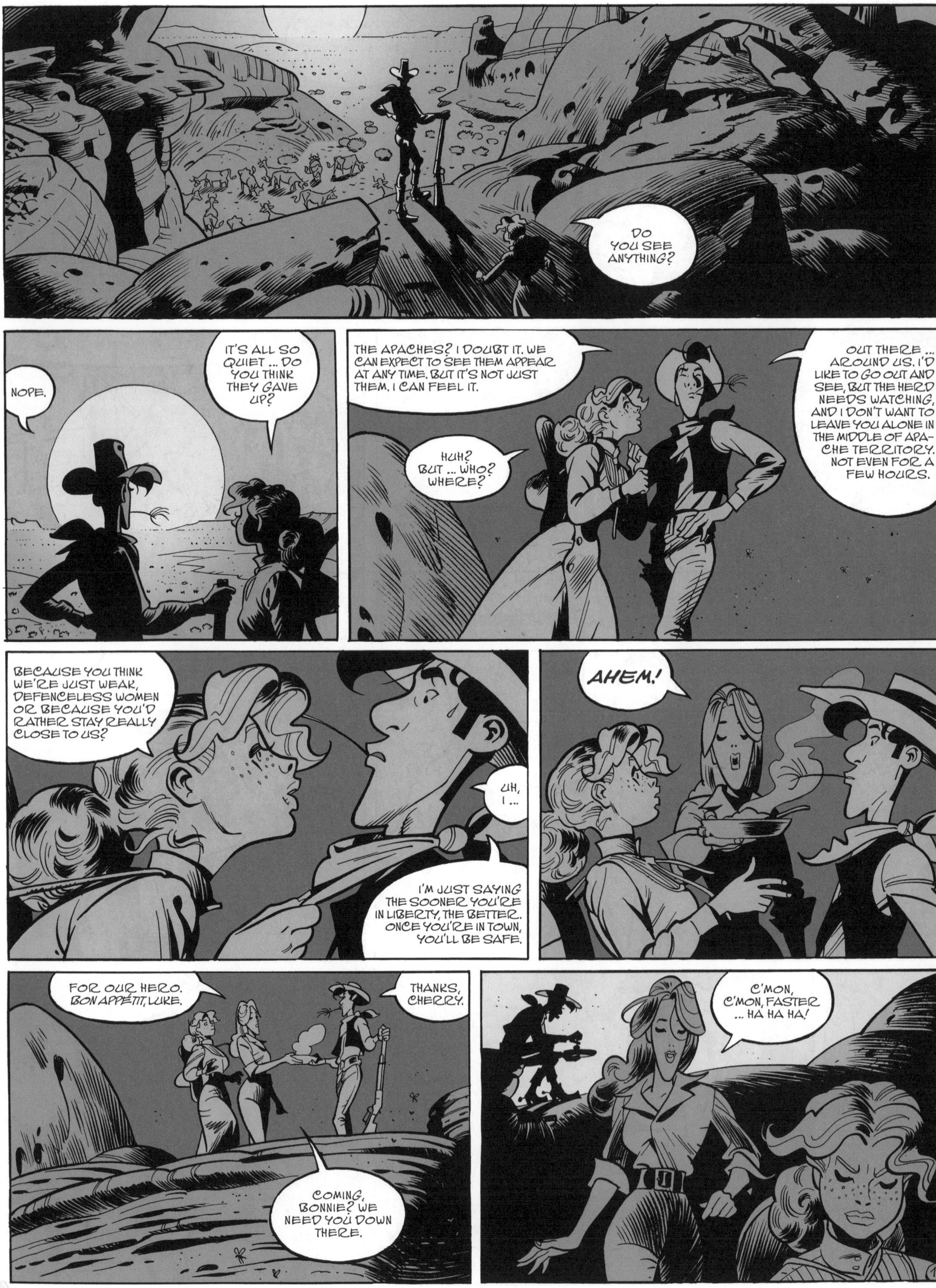
DO YOU SEE ANYTHING?
NOPE.
IT'S ALL SO QUIET ... DO YOU THINK THEY GAVE UP?
THE APACHES? I DOUBT IT. WE CAN EXPECT TO SEE THEM APPEAR AT ANY TIME. BUT IT'S NOT JUST THEM. I CAN FEEL IT.
HUH? BUT ... WHO? WHERE?
OUT THERE ... AROUND US. I'D LIKE TO GO OUT AND SEE, BUT THE HERD NEEDS WATCHING, AND I DON'T WANT TO LEAVE YOU ALONE IN THE MIDDLE OF APACHE TERRITORY. NOT EVEN FOR A FEW HOURS.
BECAUSE YOU THINK WE'RE JUST WEAK, DEFENCELESS WOMEN OR BECAUSE YOU'D RATHER STAY REALLY CLOSE TO US?
UH, I ...
I'M JUST SAYING THE SOONER YOU'RE IN LIBERTY, THE BETTER. ONCE YOU'RE IN TOWN, YOU'LL BE SAFE.
AHEM!
FOR OUR HERO. BON APPÉTIT, LUKE.
THANKS, CHERRY.
COMING, BONNIE? WE NEED YOU DOWN THERE.
C'MON, C'MON, FASTER ... HA HA HA!
18

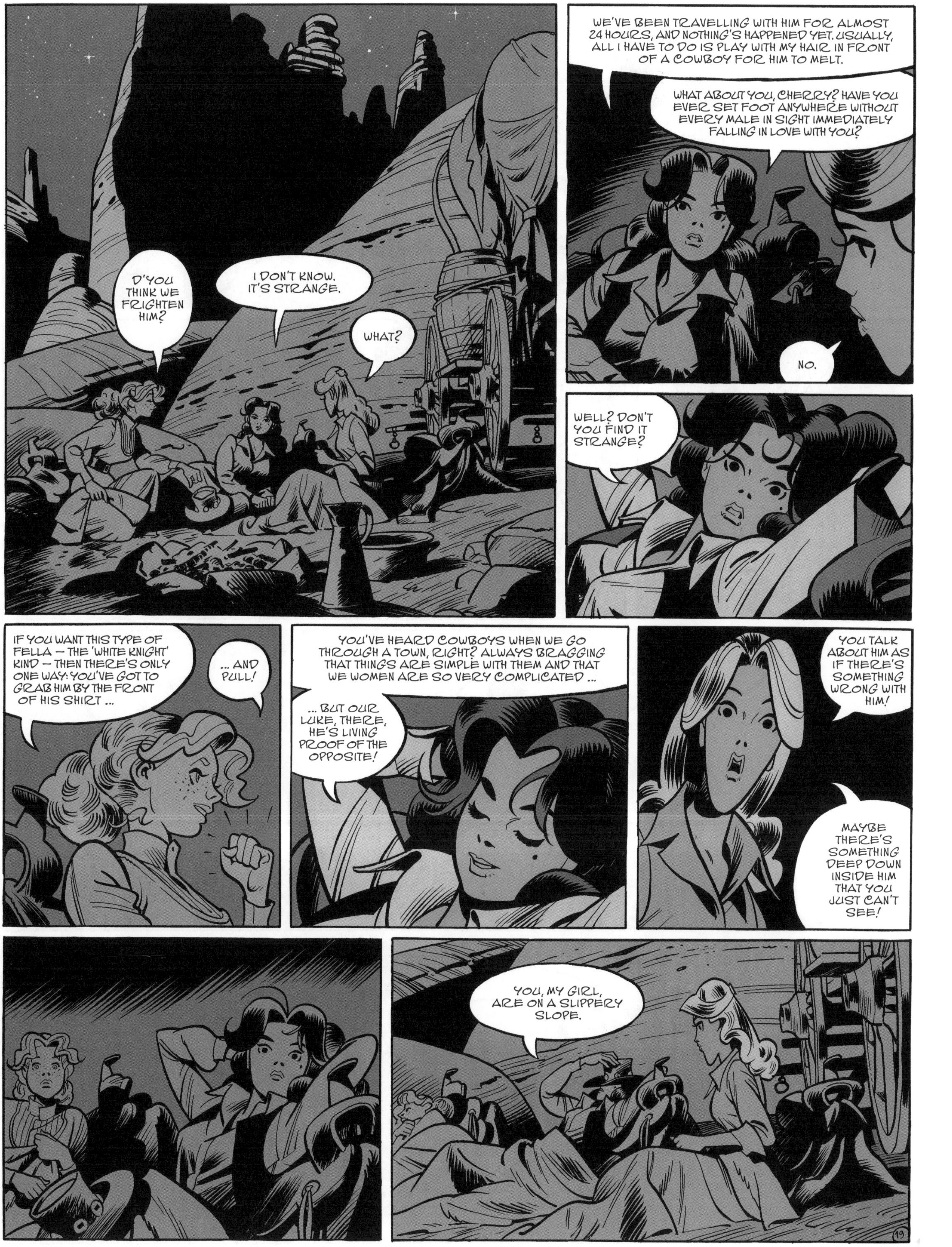
D'YOU THINK WE FRIGHTEN HIM?
I DON'T KNOW. IT'S STRANGE.
WHAT?
WE'VE BEEN TRAVELLING WITH HIM FOR ALMOST 24 HOURS, AND NOTHING'S HAPPENED YET. USUALLY, ALL I HAVE TO DO IS PLAY WITH MY HAIR IN FRONT OF A COWBOY FOR HIM TO MELT.
WHAT ABOUT YOU, CHERRY? HAVE YOU EVER SET FOOT ANYWHERE WITHOUT EVERY MALE IN SIGHT IMMEDIATELY FALLING IN LOVE WITH YOU?
NO.
WELL? DON'T YOU FIND IT STRANGE?
IF YOU WANT THIS TYPE OF FELLA – THE 'WHITE KNIGHT' KIND – THEN THERE'S ONLY ONE WAY: YOU'VE GOT TO GRAB HIM BY THE FRONT OF HIS SHIRT ...
... AND PULL!
YOU'VE HEARD COWBOYS WHEN WE GO THROUGH A TOWN, RIGHT? ALWAYS BRAGGING THAT THINGS ARE SIMPLE WITH THEM AND THAT WE WOMEN ARE SO VERY COMPLICATED ...
... BUT OUR LUKE, THERE, HE'S LIVING PROOF OF THE OPPOSITE!
YOU TALK ABOUT HIM AS IF THERE'S SOMETHING WRONG WITH HIM!
MAYBE THERE'S SOMETHING DEEP DOWN INSIDE HIM THAT YOU JUST CAN'T SEE!
YOU, MY GIRL, ARE ON A SLIPPERY SLOPE.
19

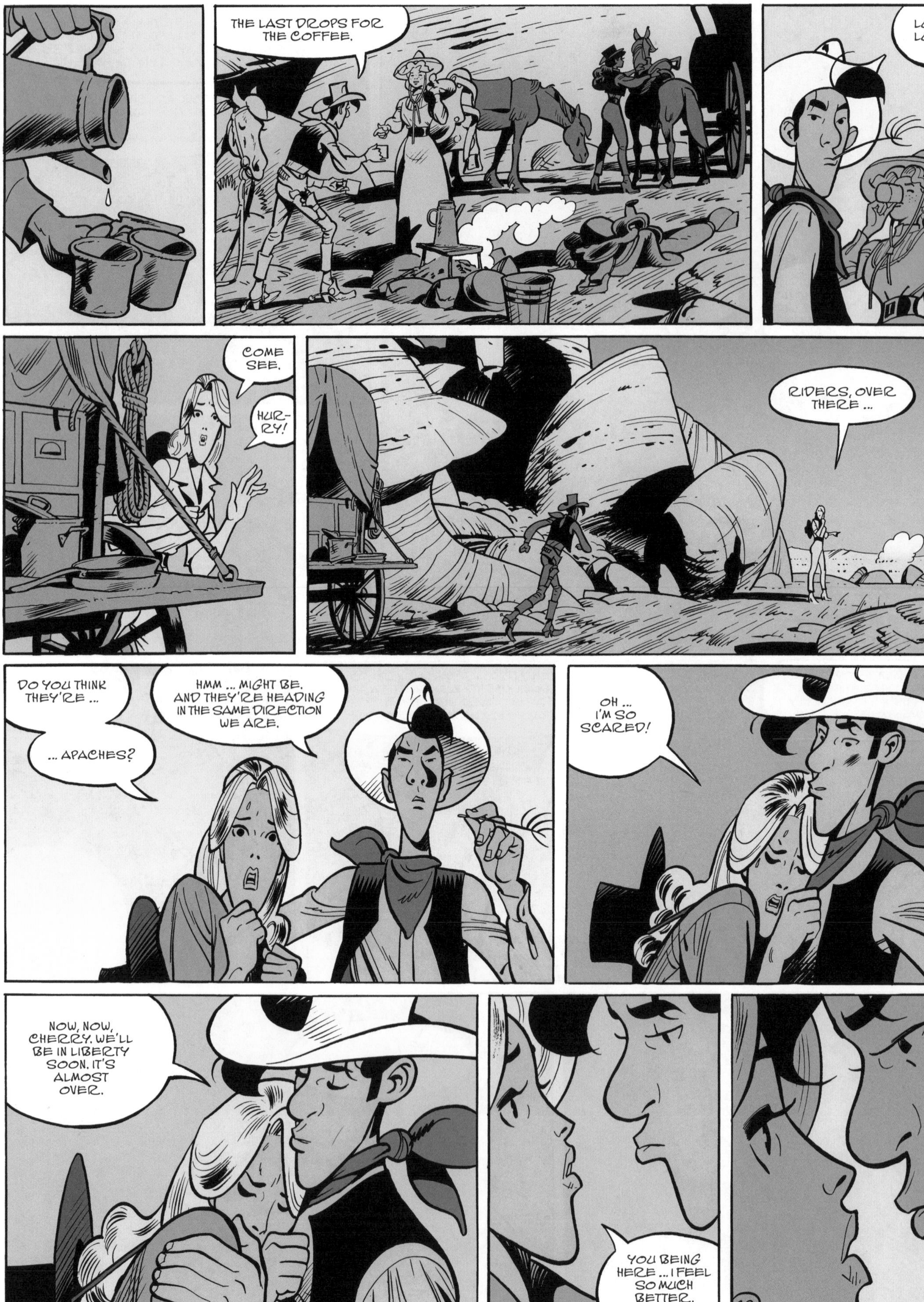

THE LAST DROPS FOR THE COFFEE.
LUKE! LUKE!
COME SEE.
HURRY!
RIDERS, OVER THERE ...
DO YOU THINK THEY'RE ...
HMM ... MIGHT BE. AND THEY'RE HEADING IN THE SAME DIRECTION WE ARE.
... APACHES?
OH ... I'M SO SCARED!
NOW, NOW, CHERRY. WE'LL BE IN LIBERTY SOON. IT'S ALMOST OVER.
YOU BEING HERE ... I FEEL SO MUCH BETTER.
20

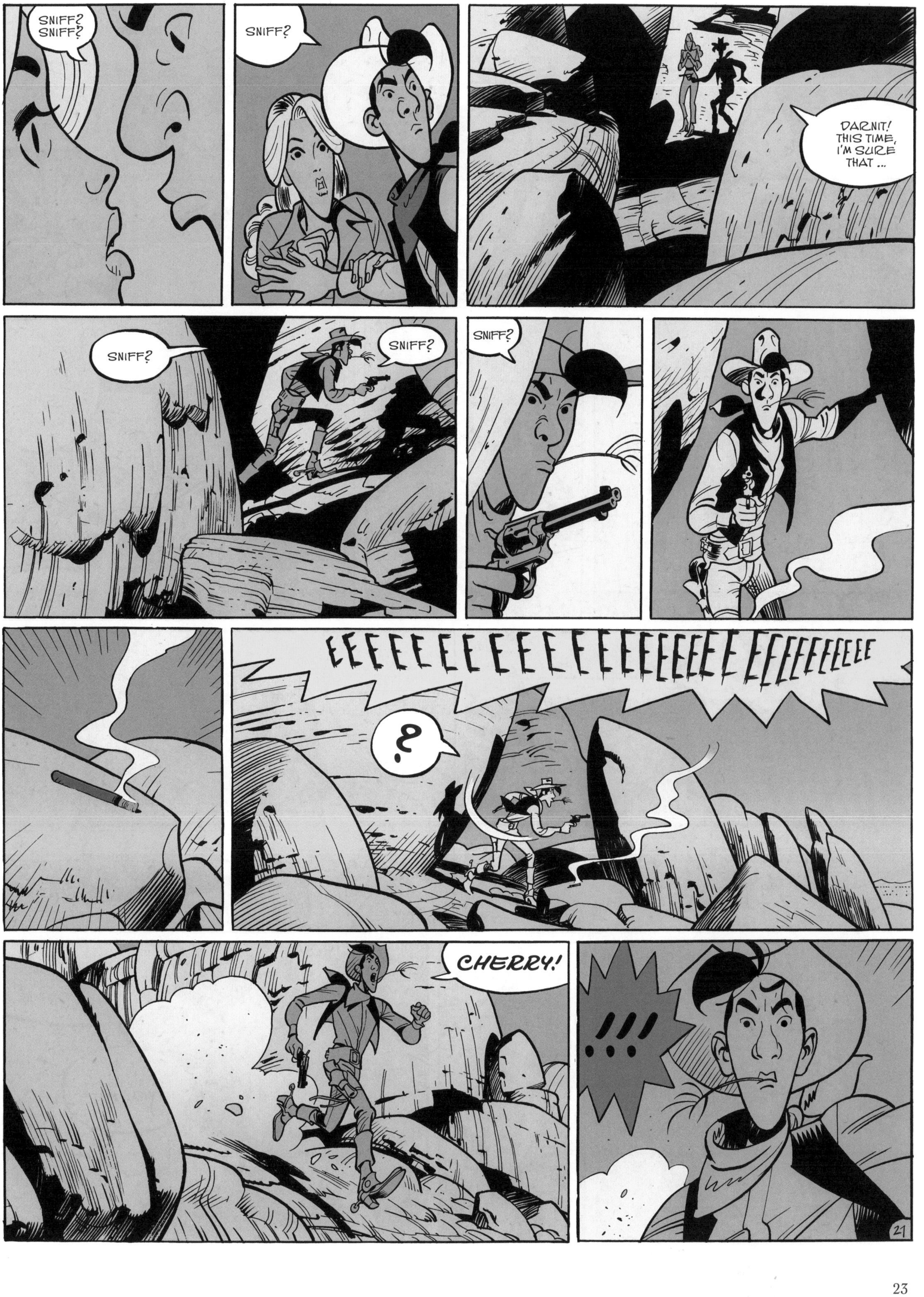
SNIFF? SNIFF?
SNIFF?
DARNIT! THIS TIME, I'M SURE THAT ...
SNIFF?
SNIFF?
SNIFF?
EEEEEEEEEEEEEEEEEEEEEEEEEEEEEE
?
CHERRY!
!!!
21

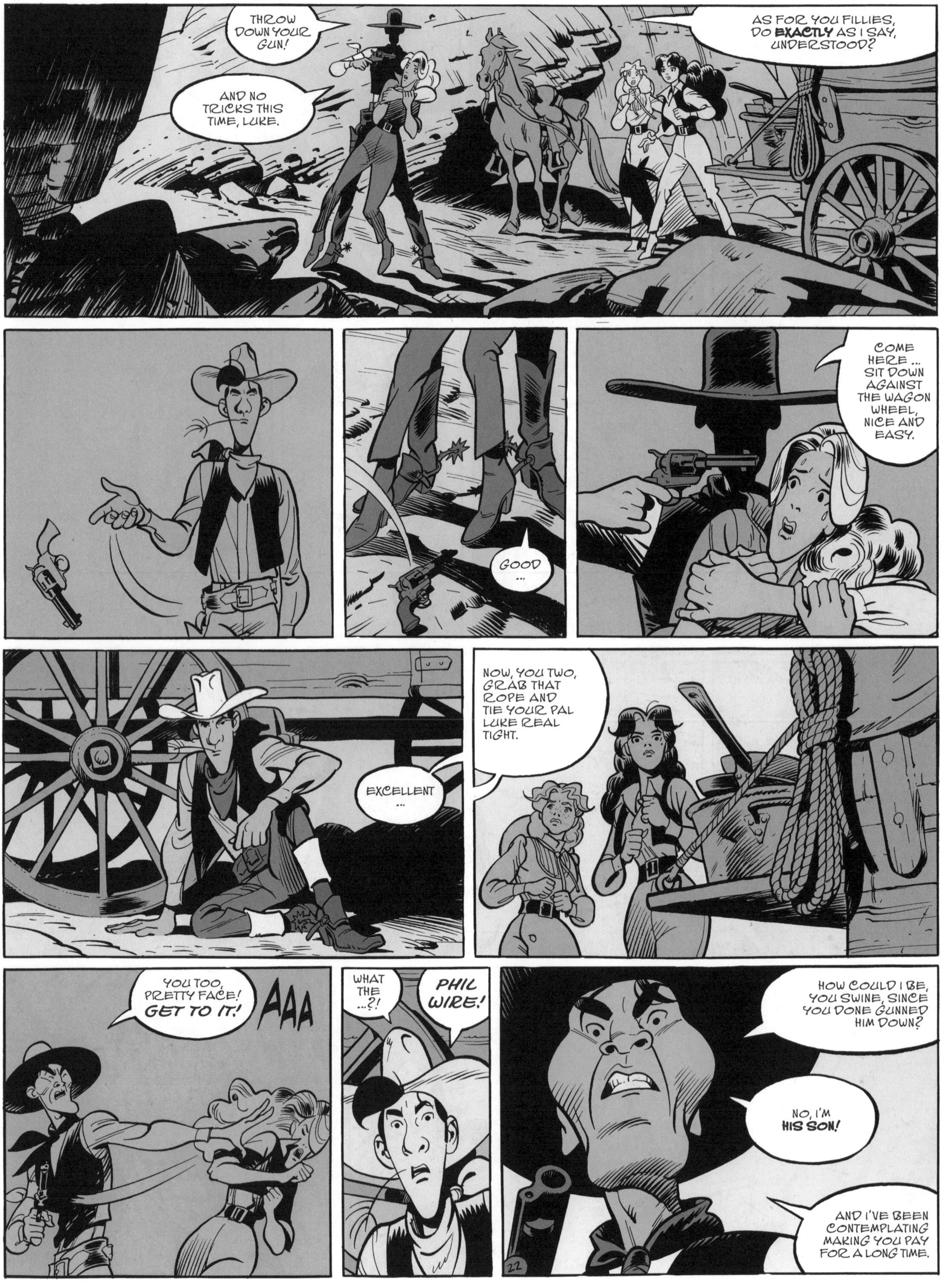
THROW DOWN YOUR GUN!
AND NO TRICKS THIS TIME, LUKE.
AS FOR YOU FILLIES, DO **EXACTLY** AS I SAY, UNDERSTOOD?
GOOD ...
COME HERE ... SIT DOWN AGAINST THE WAGON WHEEL, NICE AND EASY.
EXCELLENT ...
NOW, YOU TWO, GRAB THAT ROPE AND TIE YOUR PAL LUKE REAL TIGHT.
YOU TOO, PRETTY FACE! **GET TO IT!**
AAA
WHAT THE ...?!
PHIL WIRE!
HOW COULD I BE, YOU SWINE, SINCE YOU DONE GUNNED HIM DOWN?
NO, I'M **HIS SON!**
AND I'VE BEEN CONTEMPLATING MAKING YOU PAY FOR A LONG TIME.

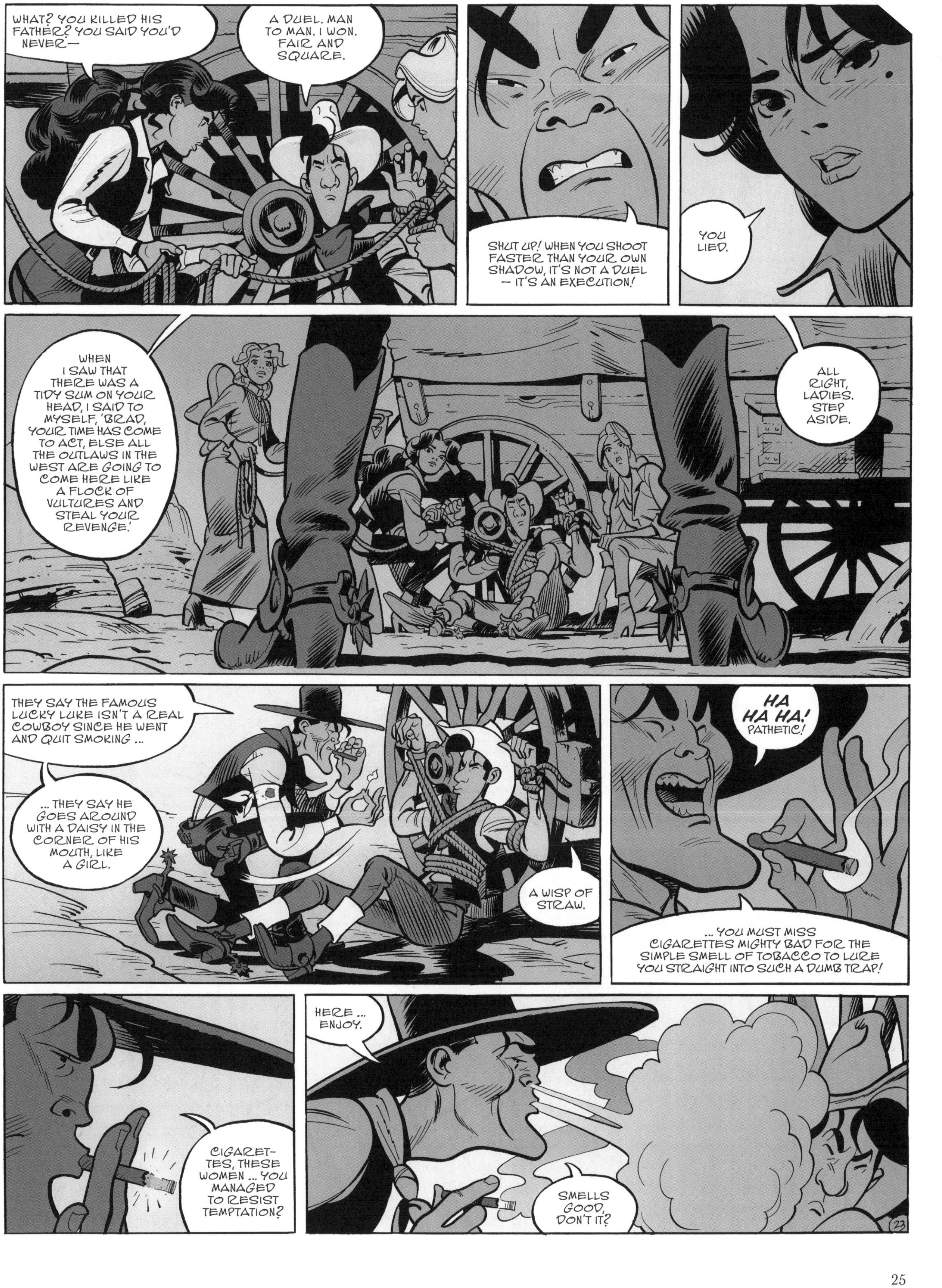

WHAT? YOU KILLED HIS FATHER? YOU SAID YOU'D NEVER—
A DUEL. MAN TO MAN. I WON. FAIR AND SQUARE.
SHUT UP! WHEN YOU SHOOT FASTER THAN YOUR OWN SHADOW, IT'S NOT A DUEL – IT'S AN EXECUTION!
YOU LIED.
WHEN I SAW THAT THERE WAS A TIDY SUM ON YOUR HEAD, I SAID TO MYSELF, 'BRAD, YOUR TIME HAS COME TO ACT, ELSE ALL THE OUTLAWS IN THE WEST ARE GOING TO COME HERE LIKE A FLOCK OF VULTURES AND STEAL YOUR REVENGE.'
ALL RIGHT, LADIES. STEP ASIDE.
THEY SAY THE FAMOUS LUCKY LUKE ISN'T A REAL COWBOY SINCE HE WENT AND QUIT SMOKING ...
... THEY SAY HE GOES AROUND WITH A DAISY IN THE CORNER OF HIS MOUTH, LIKE A GIRL.
A WISP OF STRAW.
HA HA HA! PATHETIC!
... YOU MUST MISS CIGARETTES MIGHTY BAD FOR THE SIMPLE SMELL OF TOBACCO TO LURE YOU STRAIGHT INTO SUCH A DUMB TRAP!
CIGARET-TES, THESE WOMEN ... YOU MANAGED TO RESIST TEMPTATION?
HERE ... ENJOY.
SMELLS GOOD, DON'T IT?
23

HEH HEH. I'M MORE WICKED THAN MY FATHER, MORE DANGEROUS, AND—

BRUMPFF.

DUMB-ER?

WHAT DID YOU SAY?

NOTHING. IT WAS MY HORSE. HE SAID—

WHAT? A TALKING HORSE? D'YOU THINK I'M AN IDIOT?!

BRUMPFF.

HE SAID YEP.

YOU THINK YOU CAN MOCK ME?!

YOU'RE HAVING FUN, IS THAT IT?

I CAN HAVE FUN TOO.

!!!

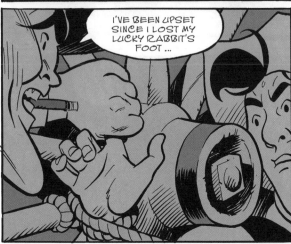

I'VE BEEN UPSET SINCE I LOST MY LUCKY RABBIT'S FOOT ...

... BUT THE TRIGGER FINGER OF THE BEST GUN-SLINGER IN THE WEST WILL MAKE A MUCH BETTER LUCKY CHARM.

THE POSTER SAID 'ALIVE', NOT 'INTACT'.

NO-O-O!

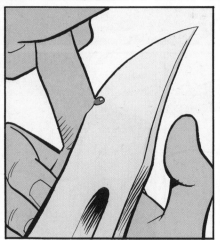

BONNG

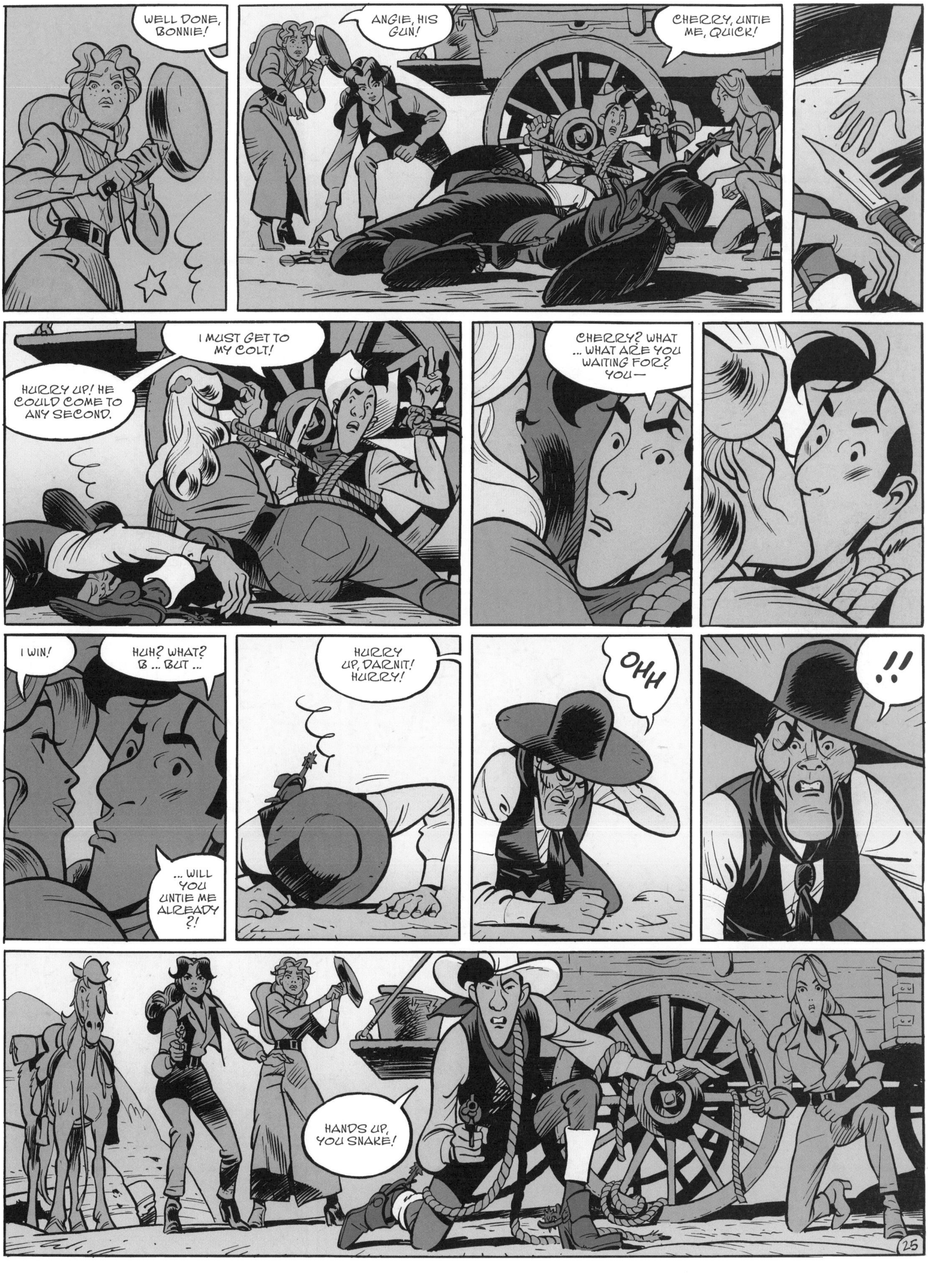
WELL DONE, BONNIE!
ANGIE, HIS GUN!
CHERRY, UNTIE ME, QUICK!
I MUST GET TO MY COLT!
HURRY UP! HE COULD COME TO ANY SECOND.
CHERRY? WHAT ... WHAT ARE YOU WAITING FOR? YOU—
I WIN!
HUH? WHAT? B ... BUT ...
... WILL YOU UNTIE ME ALREADY ?!
HURRY UP, DARNIT! HURRY!
OHH
!!
HANDS UP, YOU SNAKE!
25

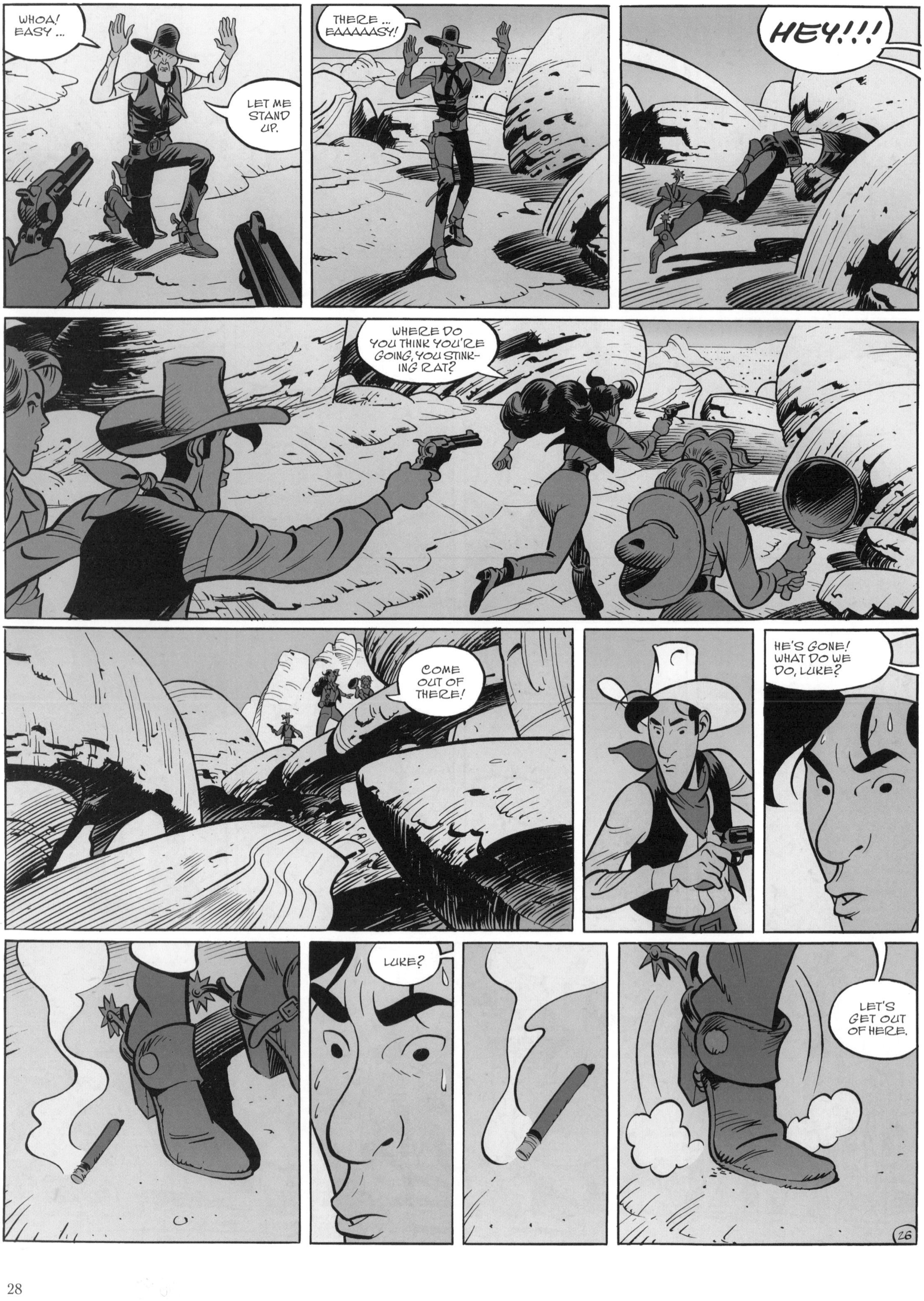
WHOA! EASY ...
LET ME STAND UP.
THERE ... EAAAAAASY!
HEY!!!
WHERE DO YOU THINK YOU'RE GOING, YOU STINK-ING RAT?
COME OUT OF THERE!
HE'S GONE! WHAT DO WE DO, LUKE?
LUKE?
LET'S GET OUT OF HERE.
26

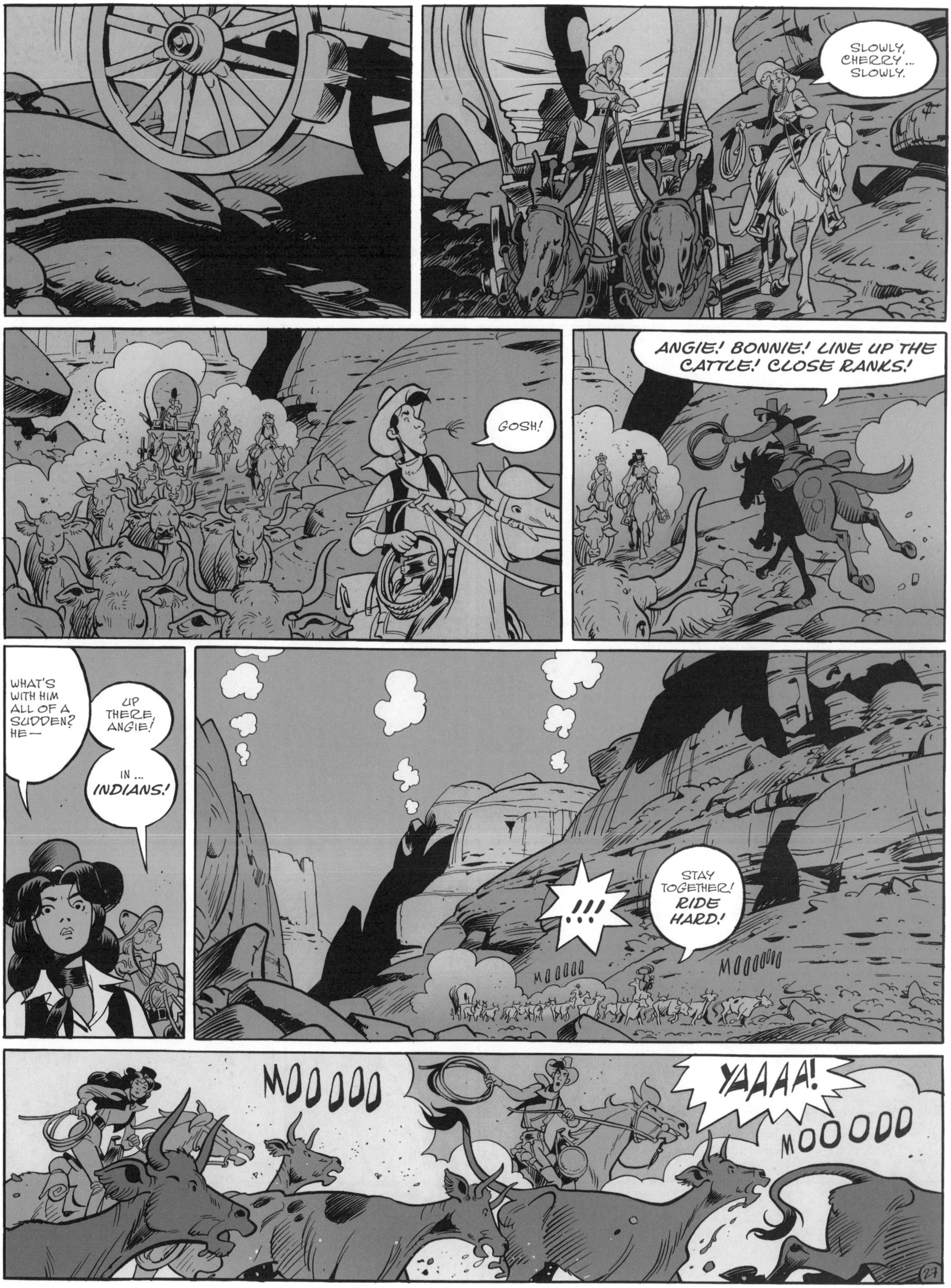
SLOWLY, CHERRY ... SLOWLY.
GOSH!
ANGIE! BONNIE! LINE UP THE CATTLE! CLOSE RANKS!
WHAT'S WITH HIM ALL OF A SUDDEN? HE—
UP THERE, ANGIE!
IN ... INDIANS!
!!!
STAY TOGETHER! RIDE HARD!
MOOOOO
MOOOOOO
MOOOOO
YAAAA!
MOOOOO

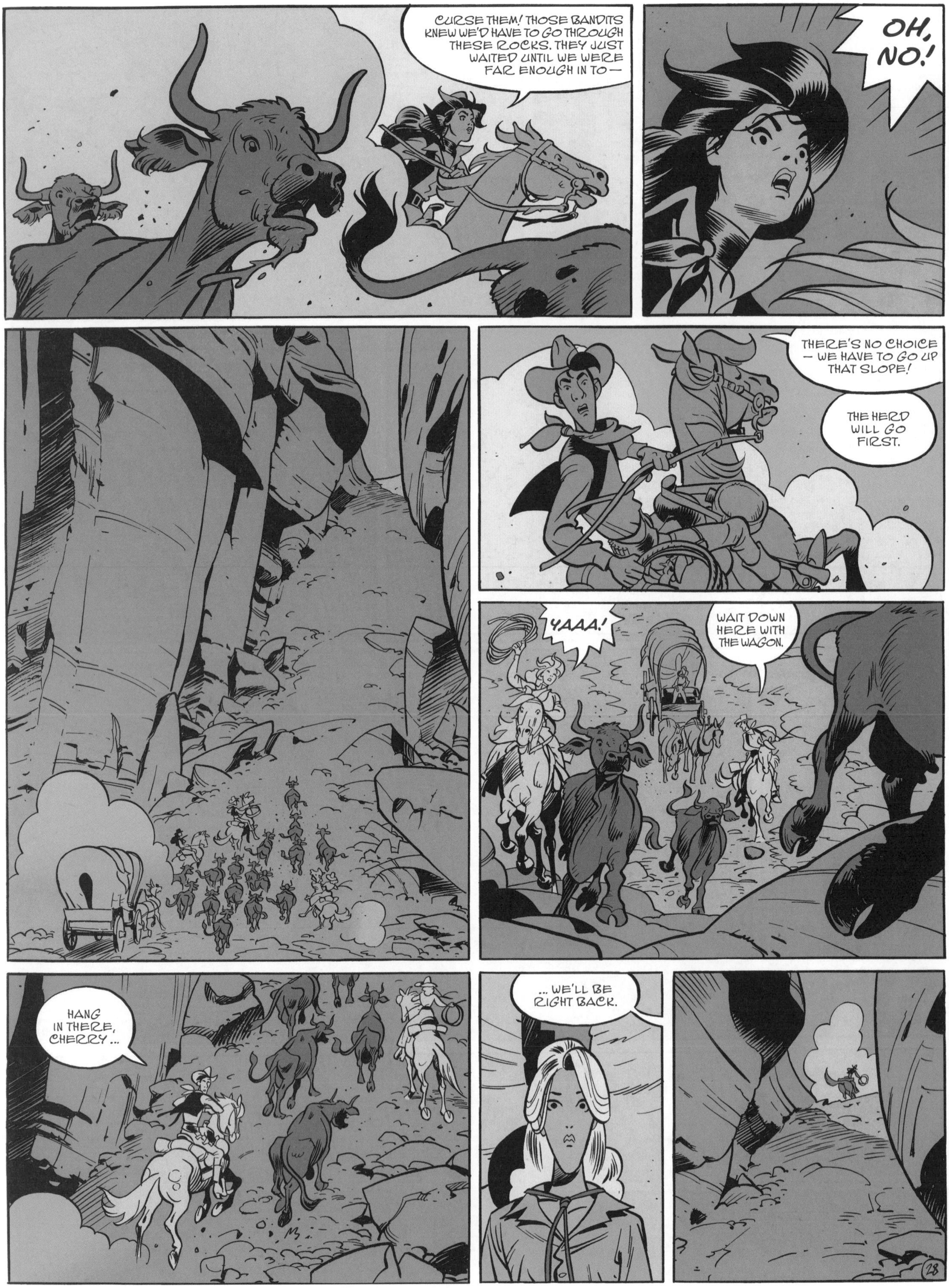
CURSE THEM! THOSE BANDITS KNEW WE'D HAVE TO GO THROUGH THESE ROCKS. THEY JUST WAITED UNTIL WE WERE FAR ENOUGH IN TO —
OH, NO!
THERE'S NO CHOICE — WE HAVE TO GO UP THAT SLOPE!
THE HERD WILL GO FIRST.
YAAA!
WAIT DOWN HERE WITH THE WAGON.
HANG IN THERE, CHERRY ...
... WE'LL BE RIGHT BACK.
28

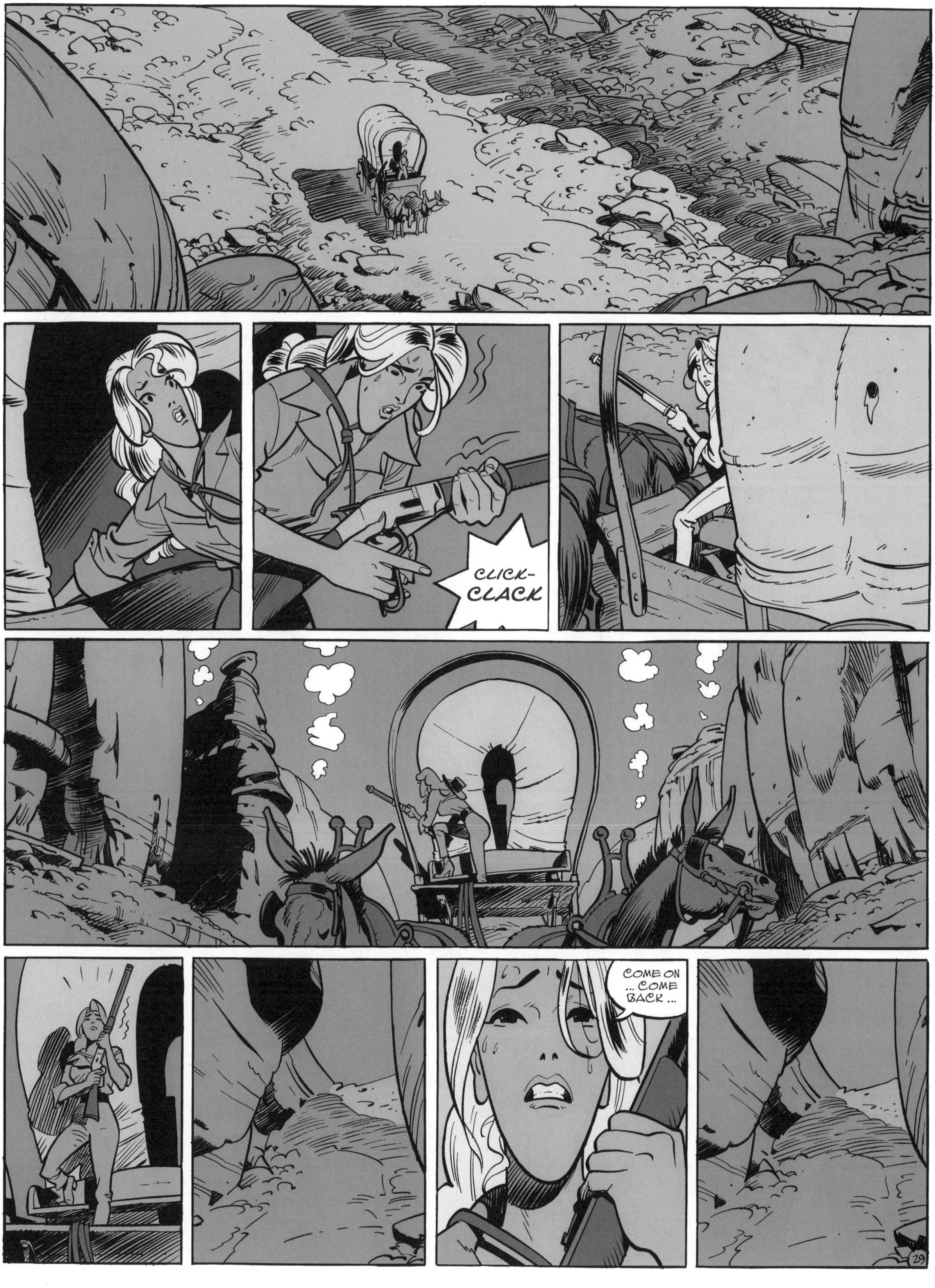
CLICK-
CLACK
COME ON ... COME BACK ...
29

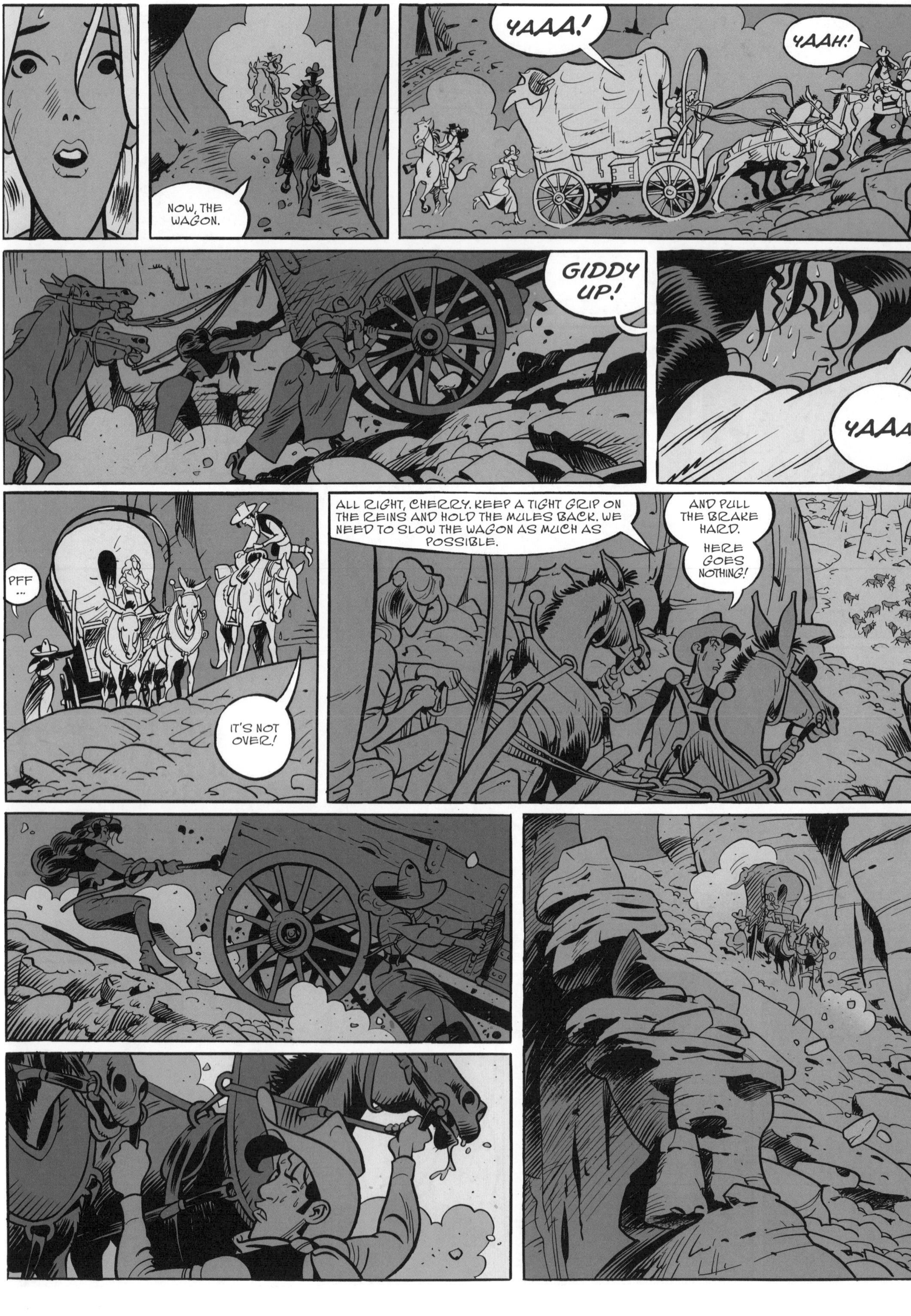
NOW, THE WAGON.
YAAA!
YAAH!
GIDDY UP!
YAAA!
PFF ...
IT'S NOT OVER!
ALL RIGHT, CHERRY. KEEP A TIGHT GRIP ON THE REINS AND HOLD THE MULES BACK. WE NEED TO SLOW THE WAGON AS MUCH AS POSSIBLE.
AND PULL THE BRAKE HARD.
HERE GOES NOTHING!
30

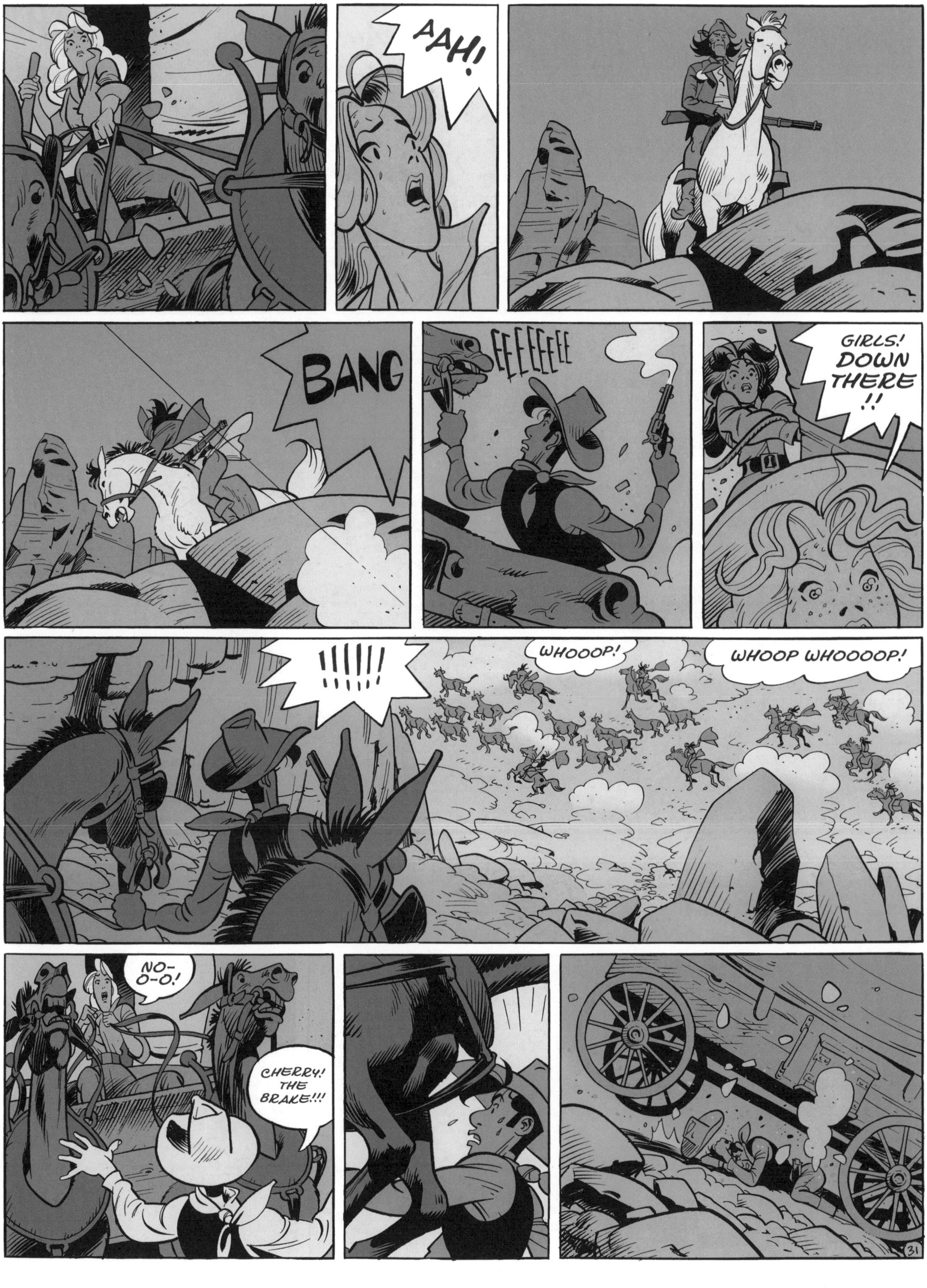
AAH!
BANG
EEEEEEEE
GIRLS! DOWN THERE !!
!!!!!!
WHOOOP!
WHOOP WHOOOOP!
NO-O-O!
CHERRY! THE BRAKE!!!
31

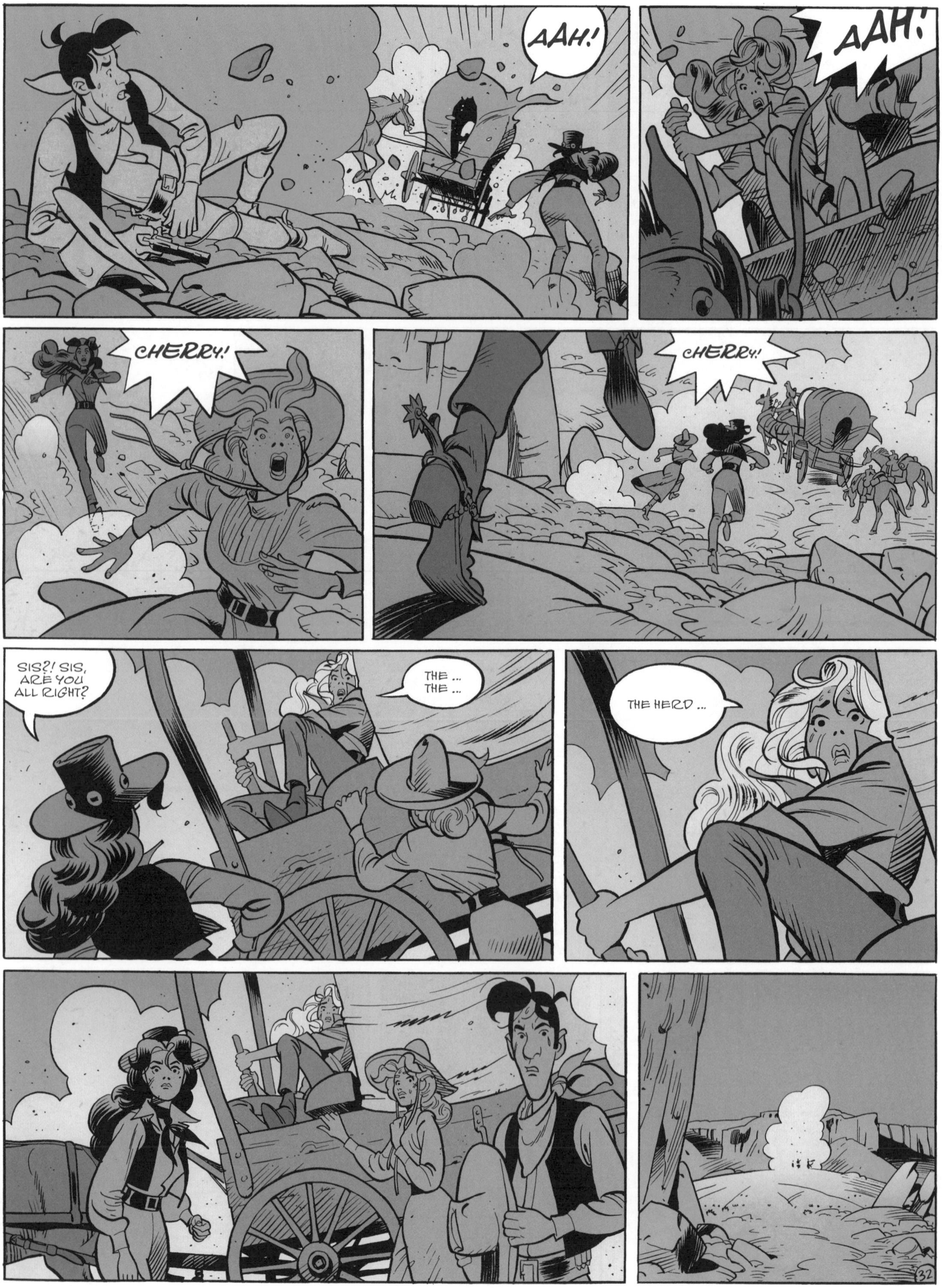
AAH!
AAH!
CHERRY!
CHERRY!
SIS?! SIS, ARE YOU ALL RIGHT?
THE ... THE ...
THE HERD ...

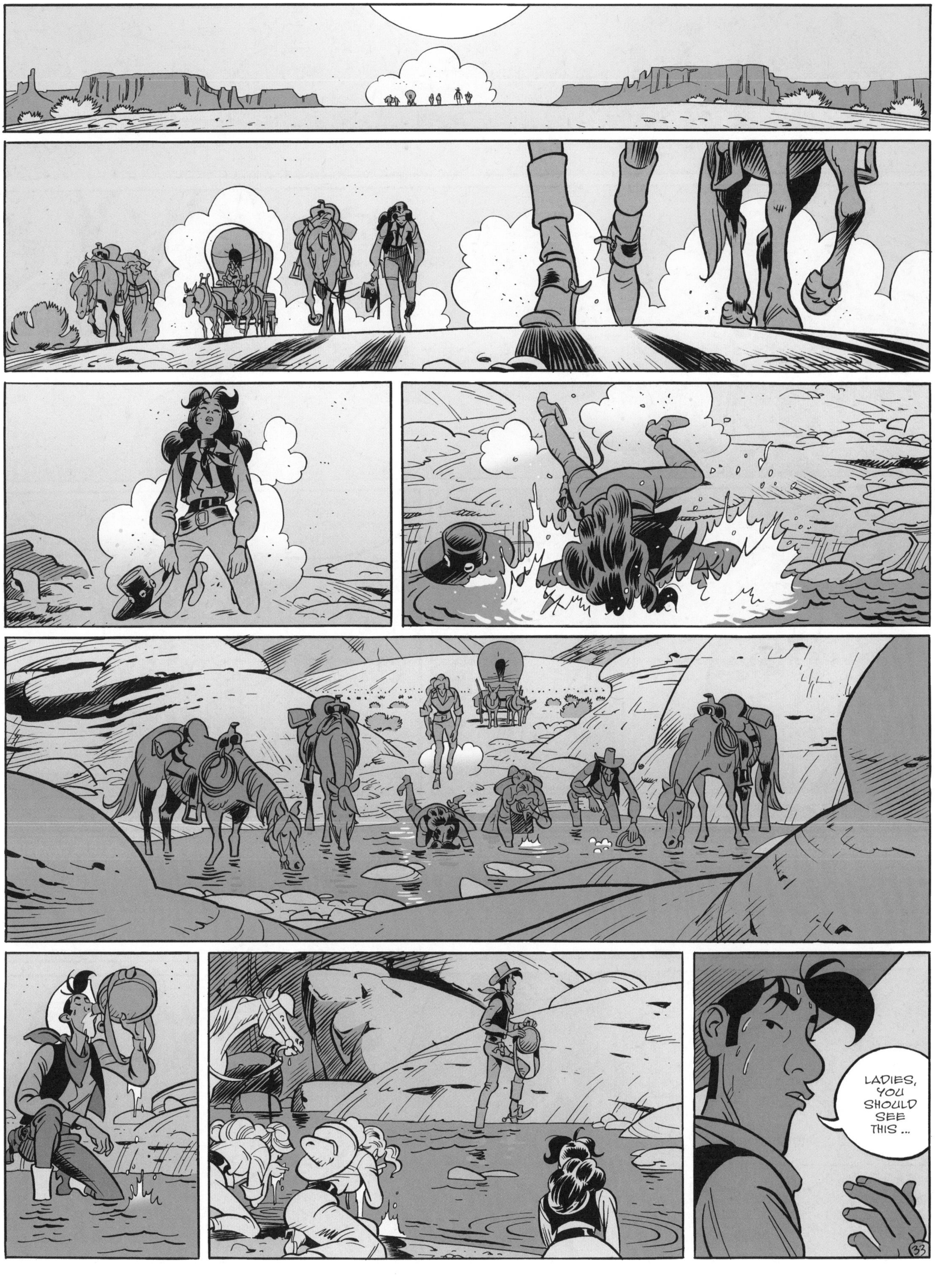
LADIES, YOU SHOULD SEE THIS ...
33

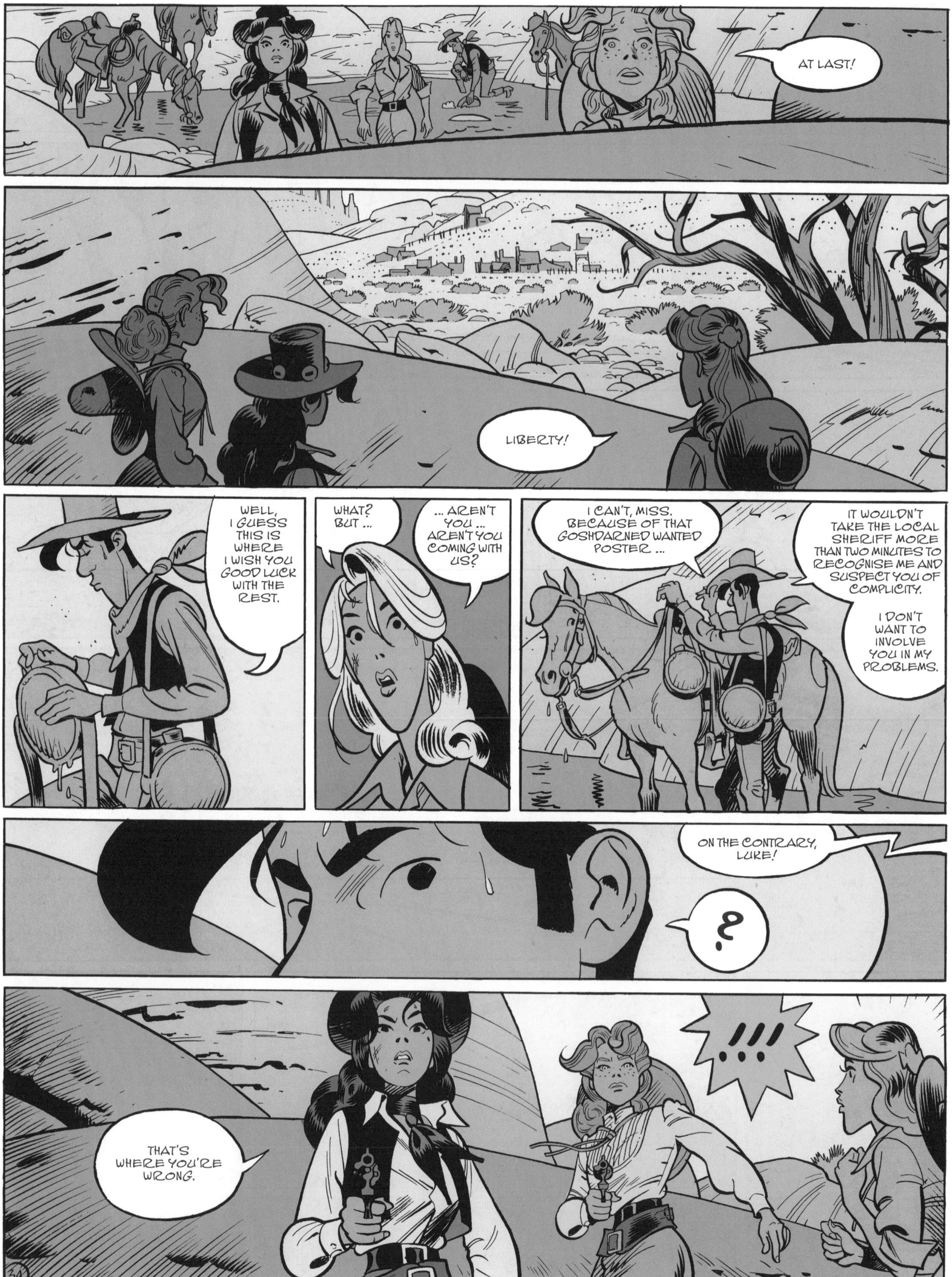
AT LAST!
LIBERTY!
WELL, I GUESS THIS IS WHERE I WISH YOU GOOD LUCK WITH THE REST.
WHAT? BUT ...
... AREN'T YOU ... AREN'T YOU COMING WITH US?
I CAN'T, MISS. BECAUSE OF THAT GOSHDARNED WANTED POSTER ...
IT WOULDN'T TAKE THE LOCAL SHERIFF MORE THAN TWO MINUTES TO RECOGNISE ME AND SUSPECT YOU OF COMPLICITY.
I DON'T WANT TO INVOLVE YOU IN MY PROBLEMS.
ON THE CONTRARY, LUKE!
?
THAT'S WHERE YOU'RE WRONG.
!!!
34

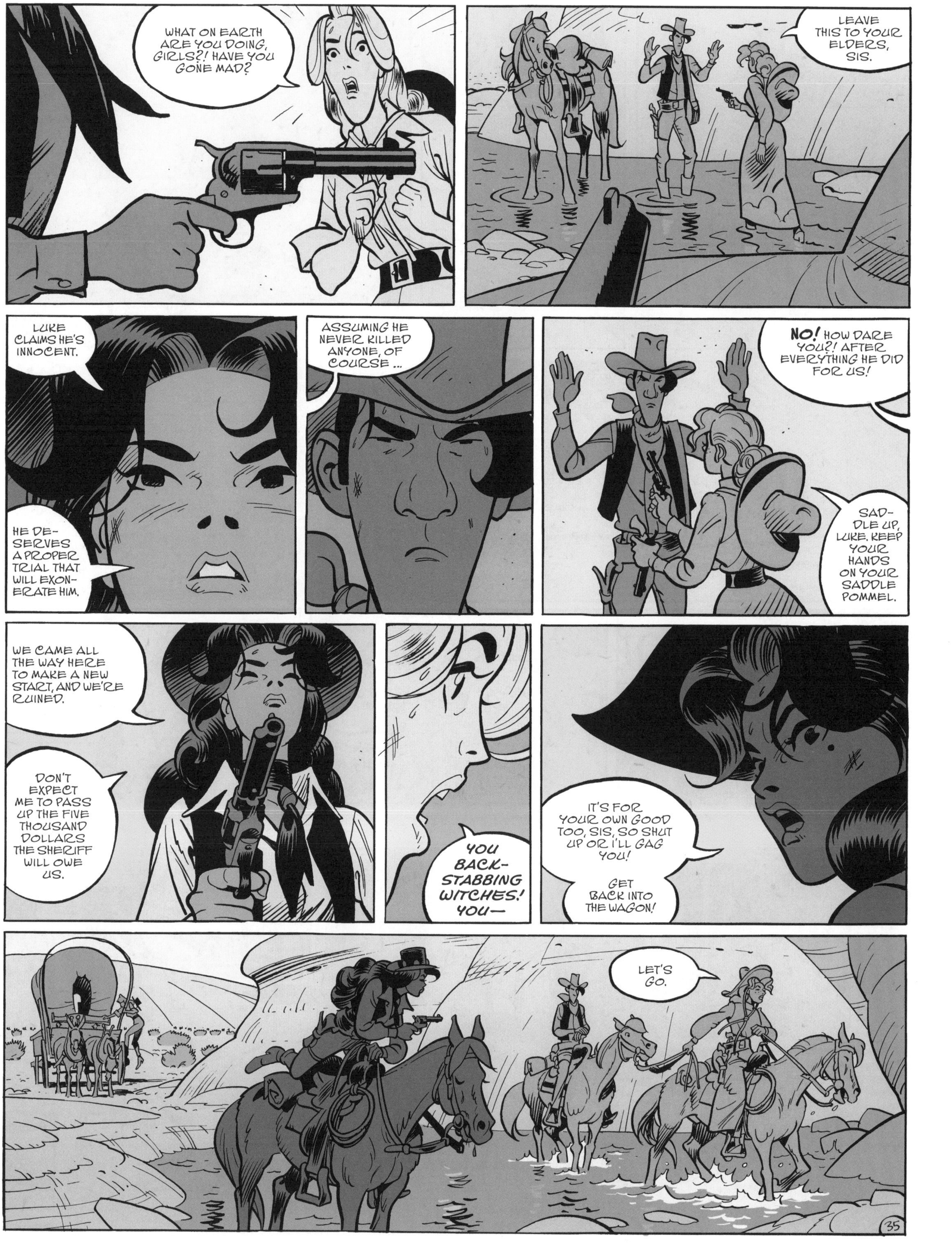
WHAT ON EARTH ARE YOU DOING, GIRLS?! HAVE YOU GONE MAD?
LEAVE THIS TO YOUR ELDERS, SIS.
LUKE CLAIMS HE'S INNOCENT.
HE DESERVES A PROPER TRIAL THAT WILL EXONERATE HIM.
ASSUMING HE NEVER KILLED ANYONE, OF COURSE ...
NO! HOW DARE YOU?! AFTER EVERYTHING HE DID FOR US!
SADDLE UP, LUKE. KEEP YOUR HANDS ON YOUR SADDLE POMMEL.
WE CAME ALL THE WAY HERE TO MAKE A NEW START, AND WE'RE RUINED.
DON'T EXPECT ME TO PASS UP THE FIVE THOUSAND DOLLARS THE SHERIFF WILL OWE US.
YOU BACK-STABBING WITCHES! YOU—
IT'S FOR YOUR OWN GOOD TOO, SIS, SO SHUT UP OR I'LL GAG YOU!
GET BACK INTO THE WAGON!
LET'S GO.
35

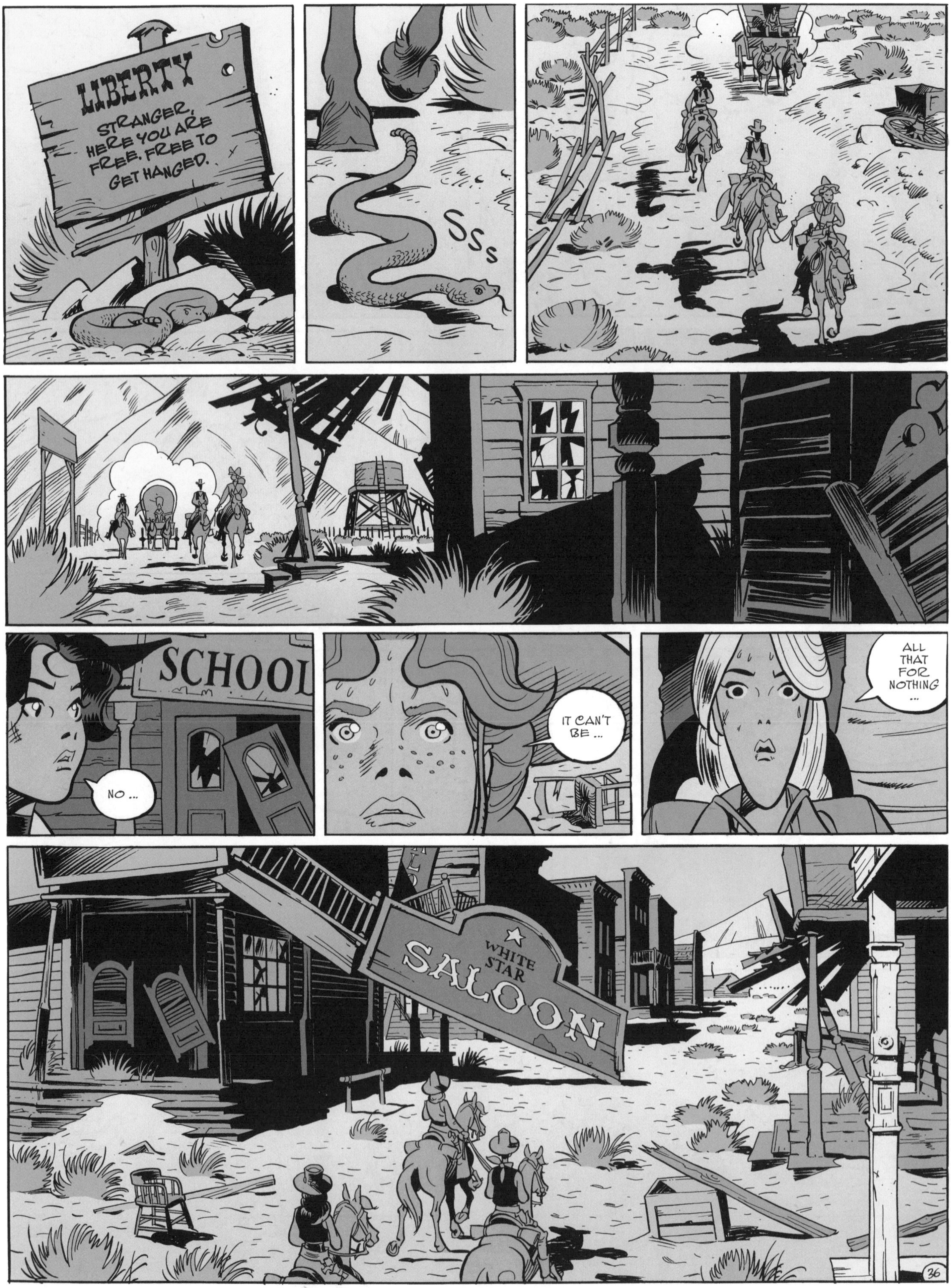
LIBERTY
STRANGER, HERE YOU ARE FREE. FREE TO GET HANGED.
SSs
NO ...
IT CAN'T BE ...
ALL THAT FOR NOTHING ...
SCHOOL
WHITE STAR SALOON
36

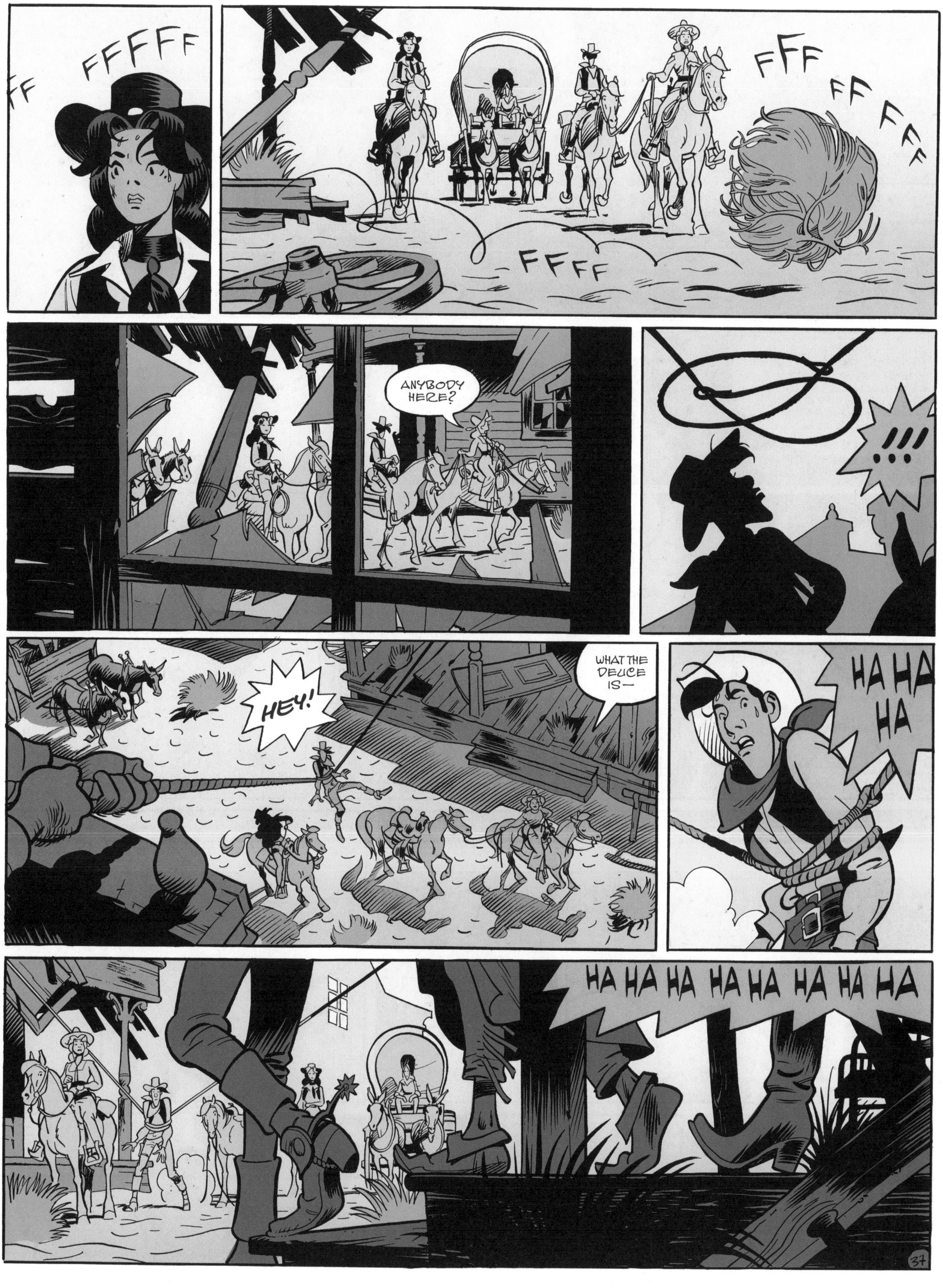
FF
FFFFF
FFF
FF
FFF
FFFF
ANYBODY HERE?
!!!
HEY!
WHAT THE DEUCE IS—
HA HA HA
HA HA HA HA HA HA HA HA HA
37

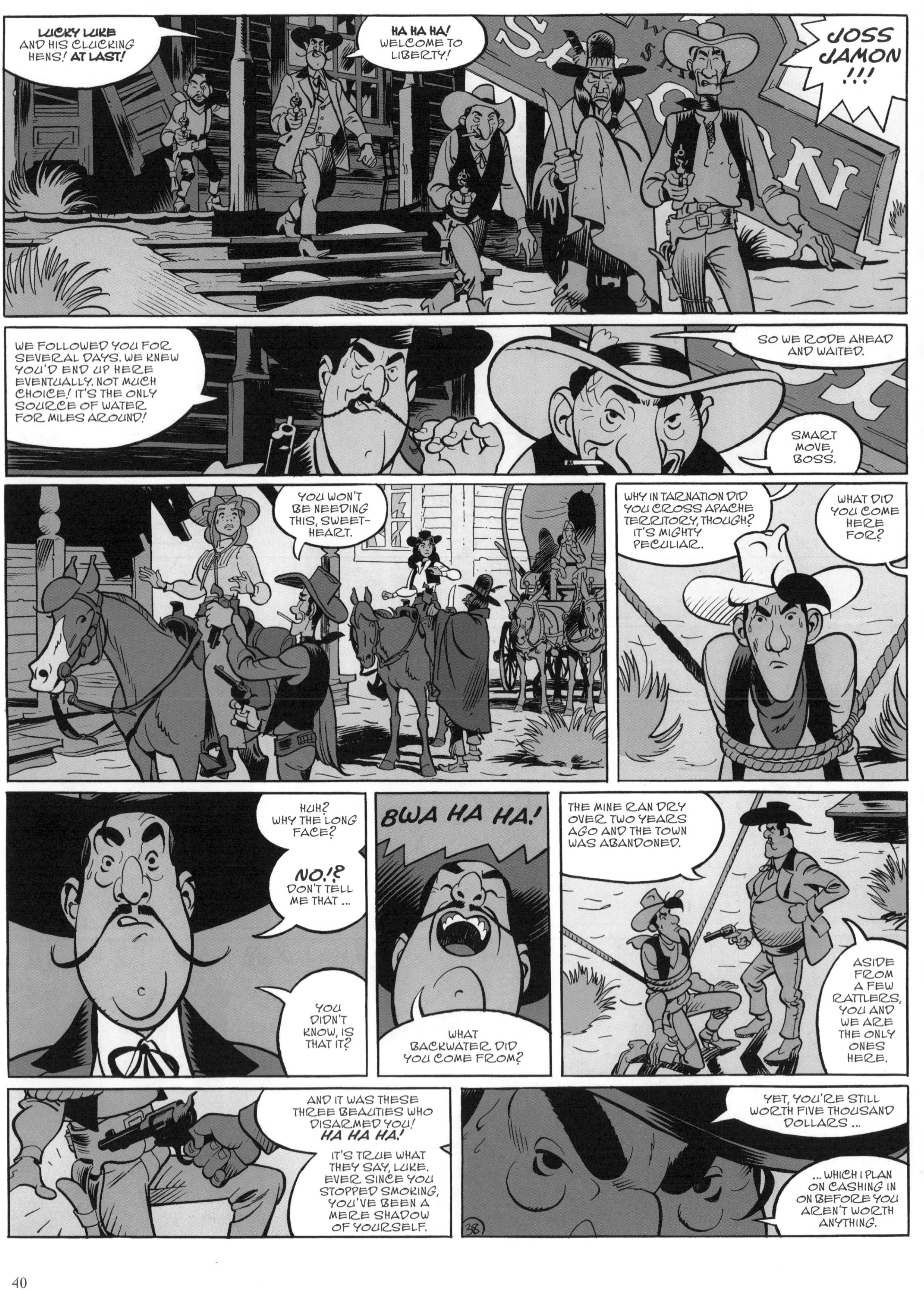
LUCKY LUKE AND HIS CLUCKING HENS! AT LAST!
HA HA HA! WELCOME TO LIBERTY!
JOSS JAMON !!!
WE FOLLOWED YOU FOR SEVERAL DAYS. WE KNEW YOU'D END UP HERE EVENTUALLY. NOT MUCH CHOICE! IT'S THE ONLY SOURCE OF WATER FOR MILES AROUND!
SO WE RODE AHEAD AND WAITED.
SMART MOVE, BOSS.
YOU WON'T BE NEEDING THIS, SWEET-HEART.
WHY IN TARNATION DID YOU CROSS APACHE TERRITORY, THOUGH? IT'S MIGHTY PECULIAR.
WHAT DID YOU COME HERE FOR?
HUH? WHY THE LONG FACE?
NO!? DON'T TELL ME THAT ...
YOU DIDN'T KNOW, IS THAT IT?
BWA HA HA!
WHAT BACKWATER DID YOU COME FROM?
THE MINE RAN DRY OVER TWO YEARS AGO AND THE TOWN WAS ABANDONED.
ASIDE FROM A FEW RATTLERS, YOU AND WE ARE THE ONLY ONES HERE.
AND IT WAS THESE THREE BEAUTIES WHO DISARMED YOU! HA HA HA!
IT'S TRUE WHAT THEY SAY, LUKE. EVER SINCE YOU STOPPED SMOKING, YOU'VE BEEN A MERE SHADOW OF YOURSELF.
YET, YOU'RE STILL WORTH FIVE THOUSAND DOLLARS ...
... WHICH I PLAN ON CASHING IN ON BEFORE YOU AREN'T WORTH ANYTHING.

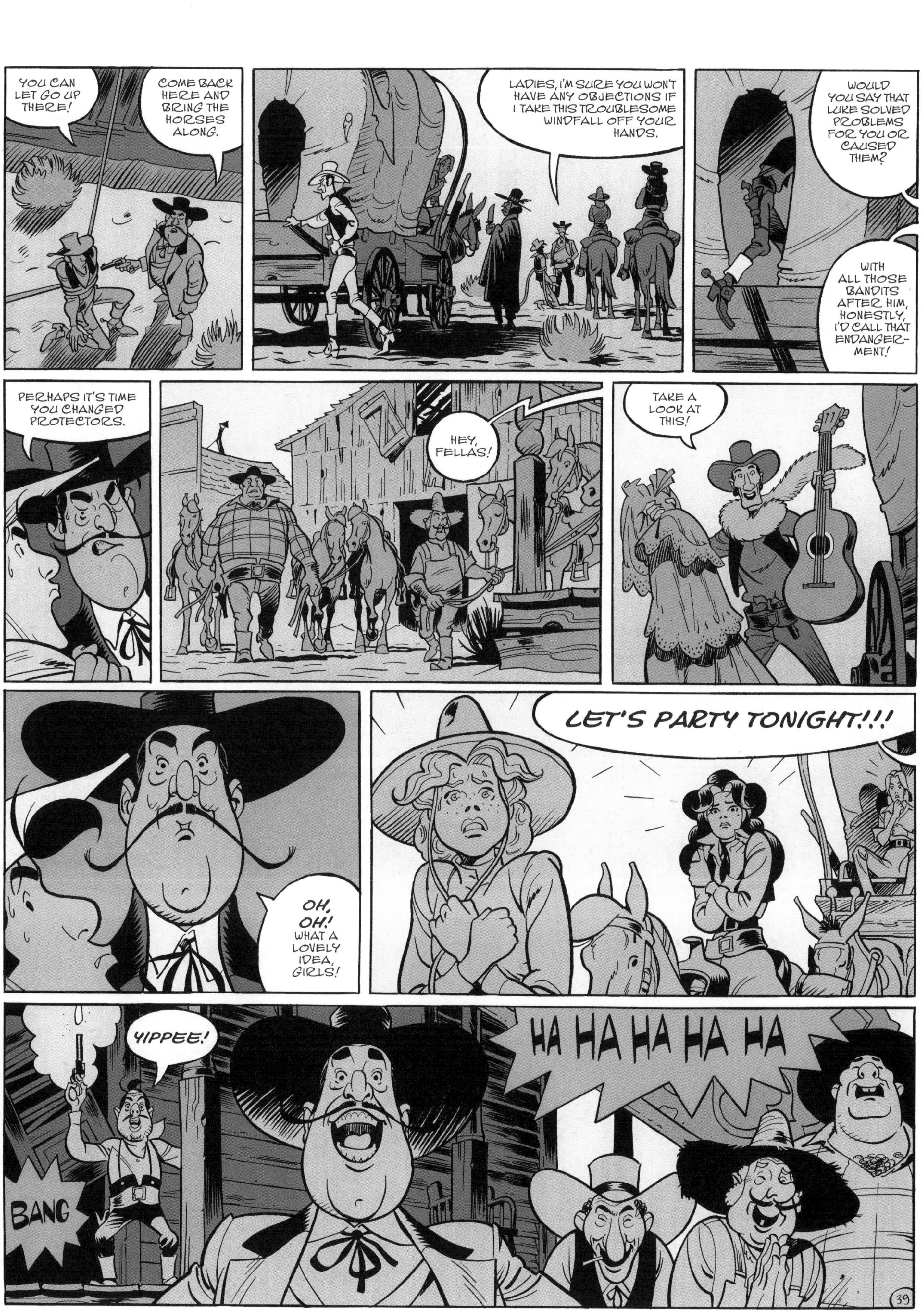
YOU CAN LET GO UP THERE!
COME BACK HERE AND BRING THE HORSES ALONG.
LADIES, I'M SURE YOU WON'T HAVE ANY OBJECTIONS IF I TAKE THIS TROUBLESOME WINDFALL OFF YOUR HANDS.
WOULD YOU SAY THAT LUKE SOLVED PROBLEMS FOR YOU OR CAUSED THEM?
WITH ALL THOSE BANDITS AFTER HIM, HONESTLY, I'D CALL THAT ENDANGERMENT!
PERHAPS IT'S TIME YOU CHANGED PROTECTORS.
HEY, FELLAS!
TAKE A LOOK AT THIS!
OH, OH! WHAT A LOVELY IDEA, GIRLS!
LET'S PARTY TONIGHT!!!
YIPPEE!
HA HA HA HA HA HA
BANG
39

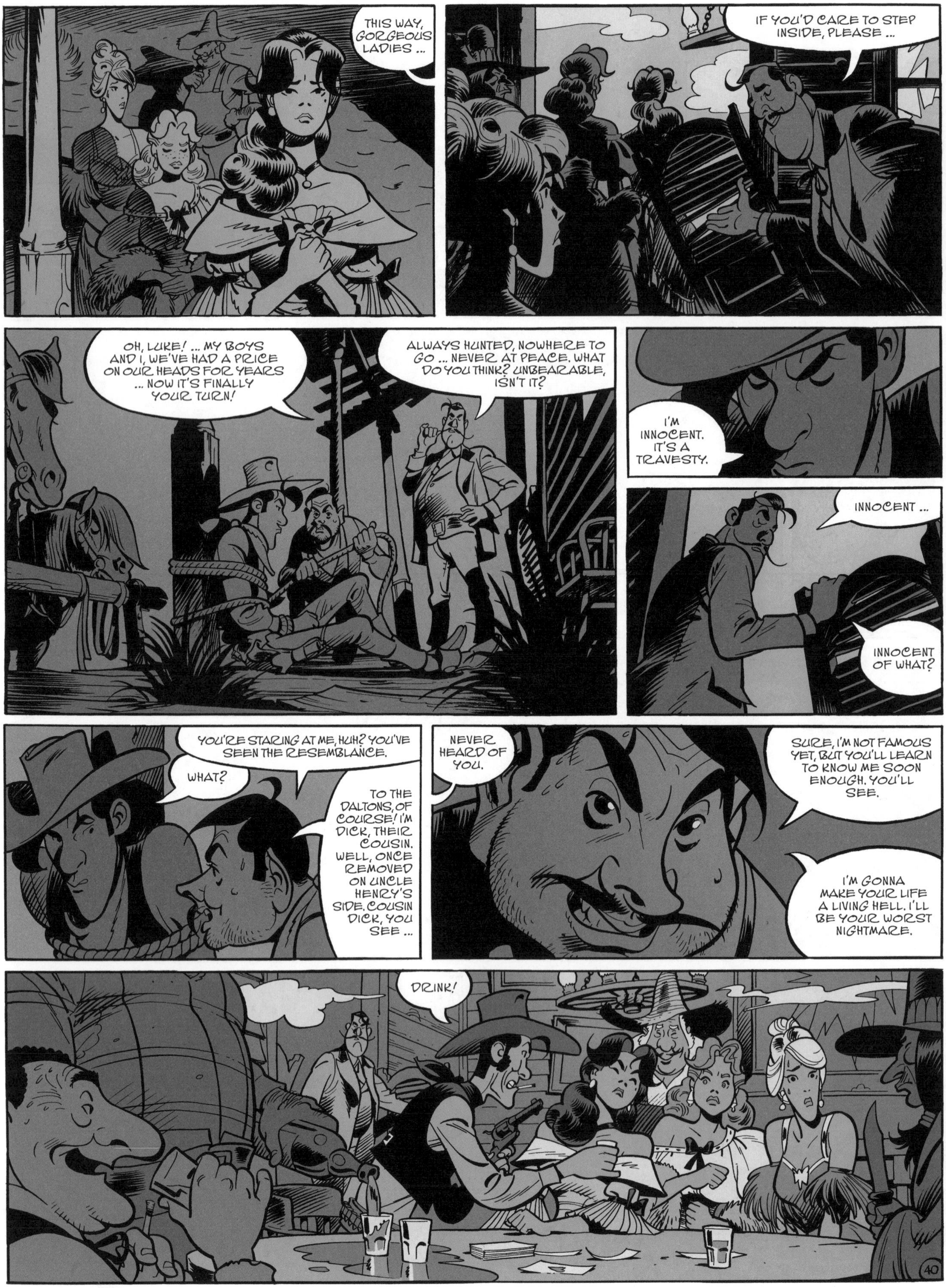
THIS WAY, GORGEOUS LADIES ...
IF YOU'D CARE TO STEP INSIDE, PLEASE ...
OH, LUKE! ... MY BOYS AND I, WE'VE HAD A PRICE ON OUR HEADS FOR YEARS ... NOW IT'S FINALLY YOUR TURN!
ALWAYS HUNTED, NOWHERE TO GO ... NEVER AT PEACE. WHAT DO YOU THINK? UNBEARABLE, ISN'T IT?
I'M INNOCENT. IT'S A TRAVESTY.
INNOCENT ...
INNOCENT OF WHAT?
YOU'RE STARING AT ME, HUH? YOU'VE SEEN THE RESEMBLANCE.
WHAT?
TO THE DALTONS, OF COURSE! I'M DICK, THEIR COUSIN. WELL, ONCE REMOVED ON UNCLE HENRY'S SIDE. COUSIN DICK, YOU SEE ...
NEVER HEARD OF YOU.
SURE, I'M NOT FAMOUS YET, BUT YOU'LL LEARN TO KNOW ME SOON ENOUGH. YOU'LL SEE.
I'M GONNA MAKE YOUR LIFE A LIVING HELL. I'LL BE YOUR WORST NIGHTMARE.
DRINK!

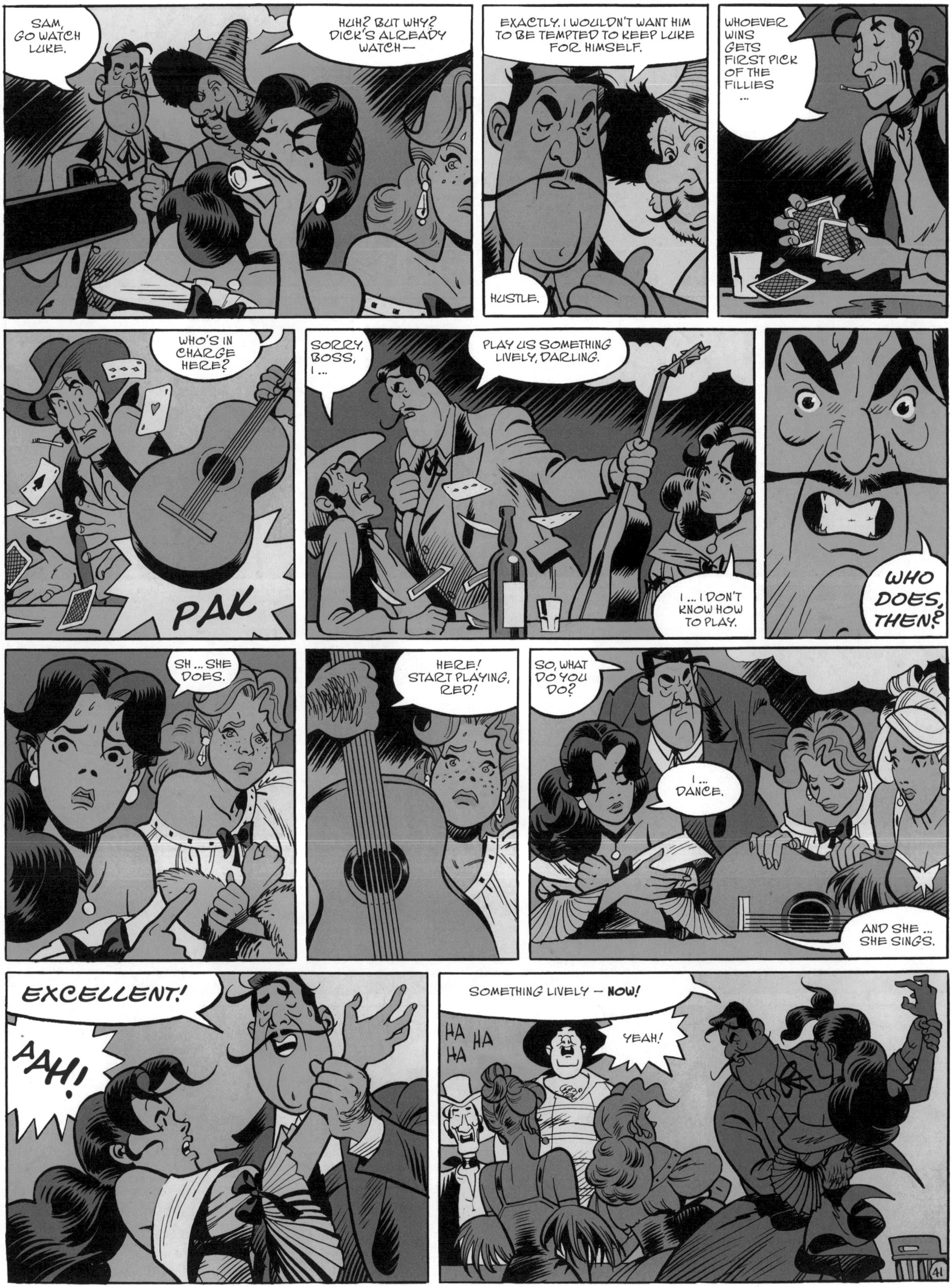
SAM, GO WATCH LUKE.
HUH? BUT WHY? DICK'S ALREADY WATCH —
EXACTLY. I WOULDN'T WANT HIM TO BE TEMPTED TO KEEP LUKE FOR HIMSELF.
HUSTLE.
WHOEVER WINS GETS FIRST PICK OF THE FILLIES ...
WHO'S IN CHARGE HERE?
PAK
SORRY, BOSS, I ...
PLAY US SOMETHING LIVELY, DARLING.
I ... I DON'T KNOW HOW TO PLAY.
WHO DOES, THEN?
SH ... SHE DOES.
HERE! START PLAYING, RED!
SO, WHAT DO YOU DO?
I ... DANCE.
AND SHE ... SHE SINGS.
EXCELLENT!
AAH!
SOMETHING LIVELY — NOW!
HA HA HA
YEAH!
41

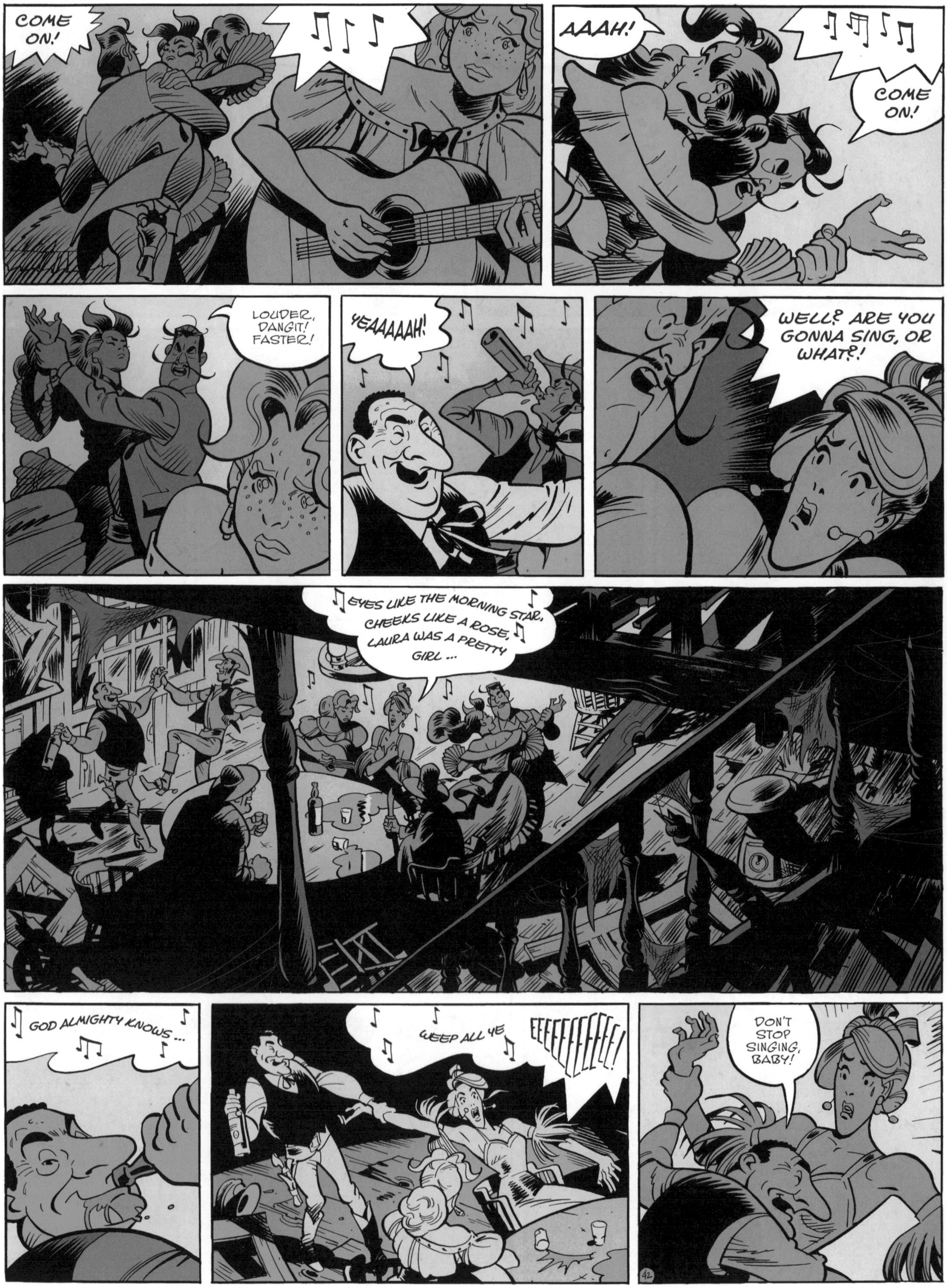
COME ON!
AAAH!
COME ON!
LOUDER, DANGIT! FASTER!
YEAAAAAH!
WELL? ARE YOU GONNA SING, OR WHAT?!
EYES LIKE THE MORNING STAR, CHEEKS LIKE A ROSE, LAURA WAS A PRETTY GIRL ...
GOD ALMIGHTY KNOWS ...
WEEP ALL YE
EEEEEEEEEEE!
DON'T STOP SINGING, BABY!

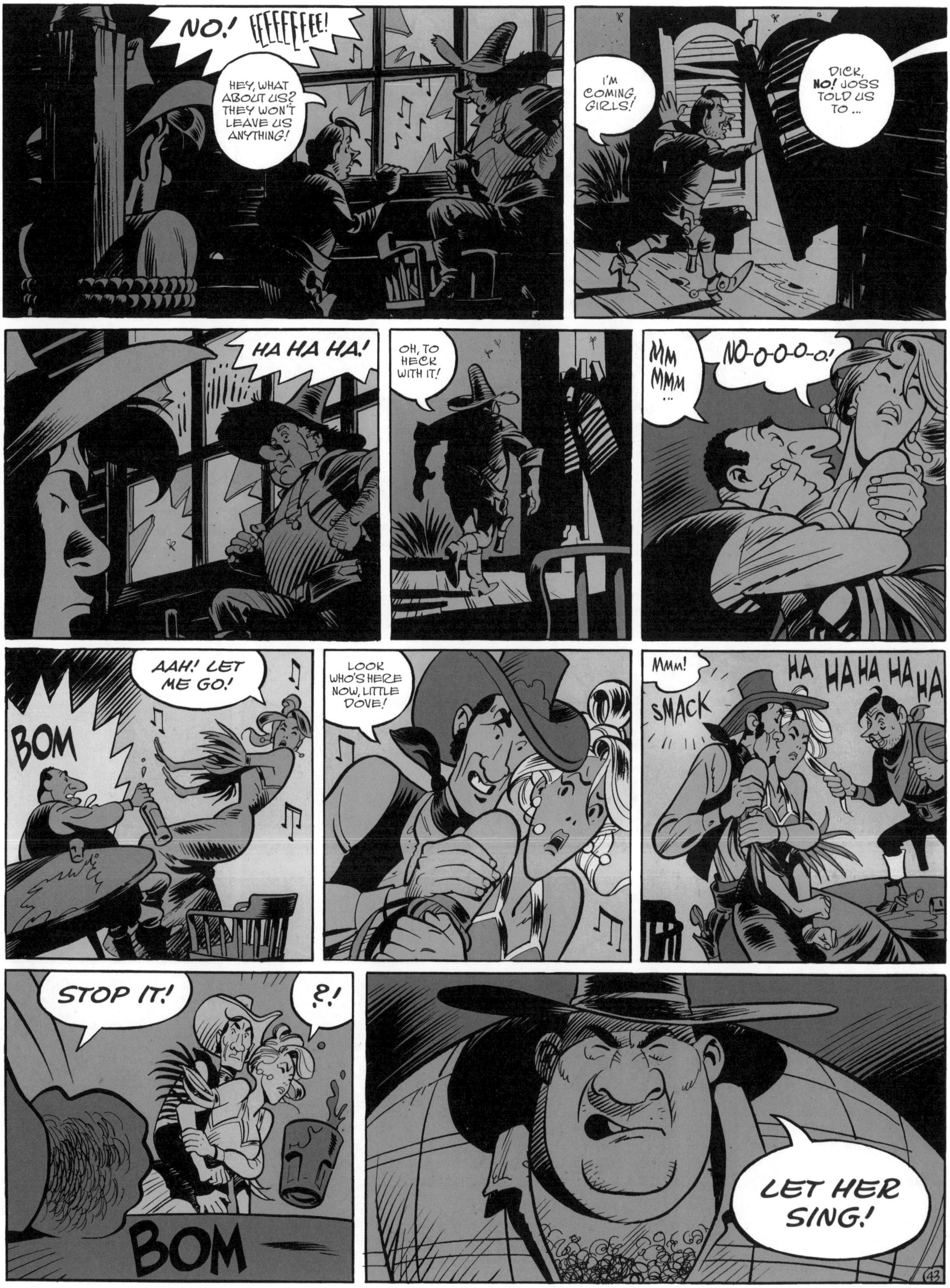
NO! EEEEEEEEE!
HEY, WHAT ABOUT US? THEY WON'T LEAVE US ANYTHING!
I'M COMING, GIRLS!
DICK, NO! JOSS TOLD US TO ...
HA HA HA!
OH, TO HECK WITH IT!
MM MMM ...
NO-O-O-O-O!
AAH! LET ME GO!
BOM
LOOK WHO'S HERE NOW, LITTLE DOVE!
MMM!
SMACK
HA HA HA HA HA HA
STOP IT!
?!
BOM
LET HER SING!
43

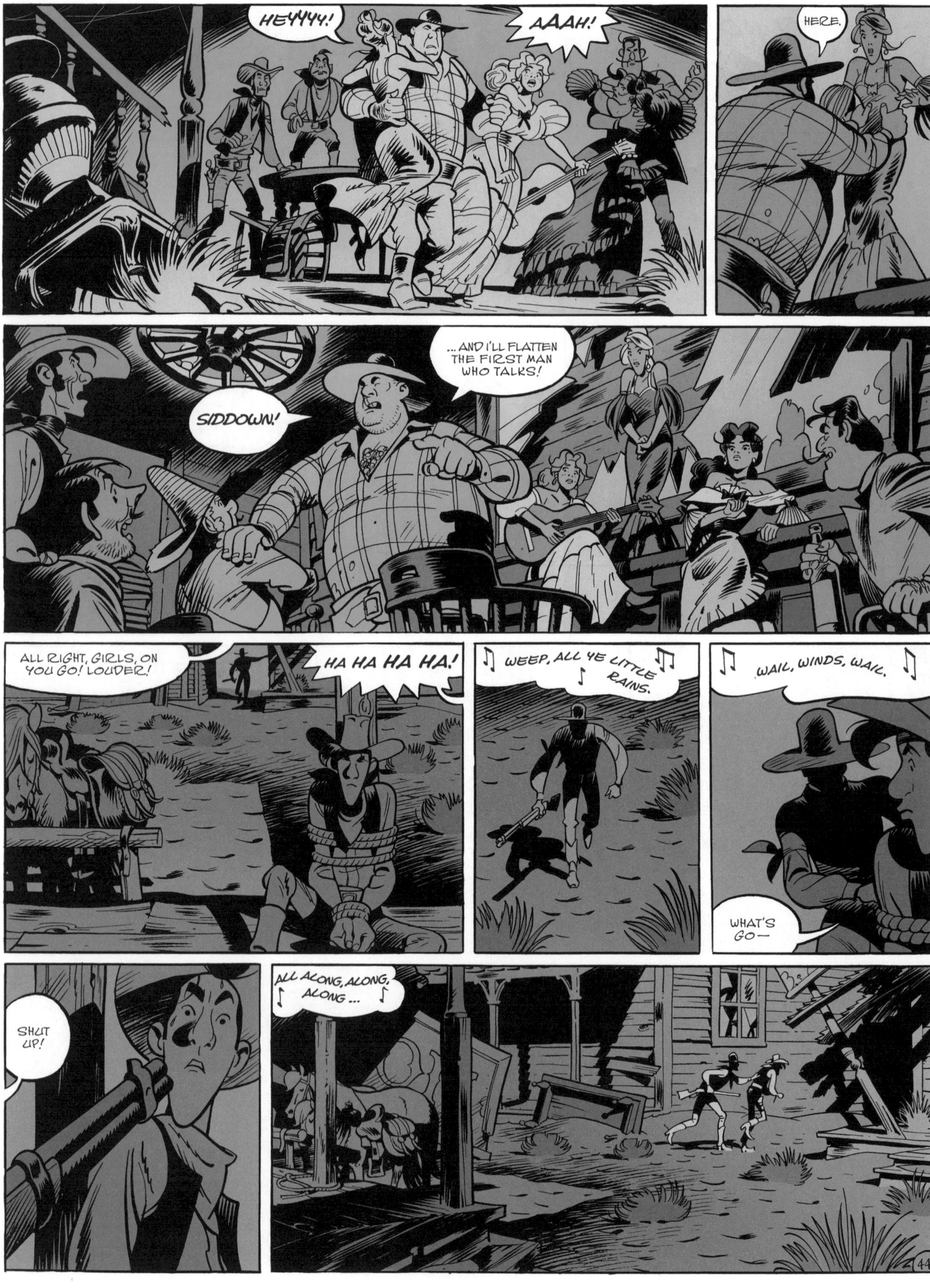

HEYYYY!
AAAH!
HERE.
SIDDOWN!
...AND I'LL FLATTEN THE FIRST MAN WHO TALKS!
ALL RIGHT, GIRLS, ON YOU GO! LOUDER!
HA HA HA HA!
WEEP, ALL YE LITTLE RAINS.
WAIL, WINDS, WAIL.
WHAT'S GO—
SHUT UP!
ALL ALONG, ALONG, ALONG...
44

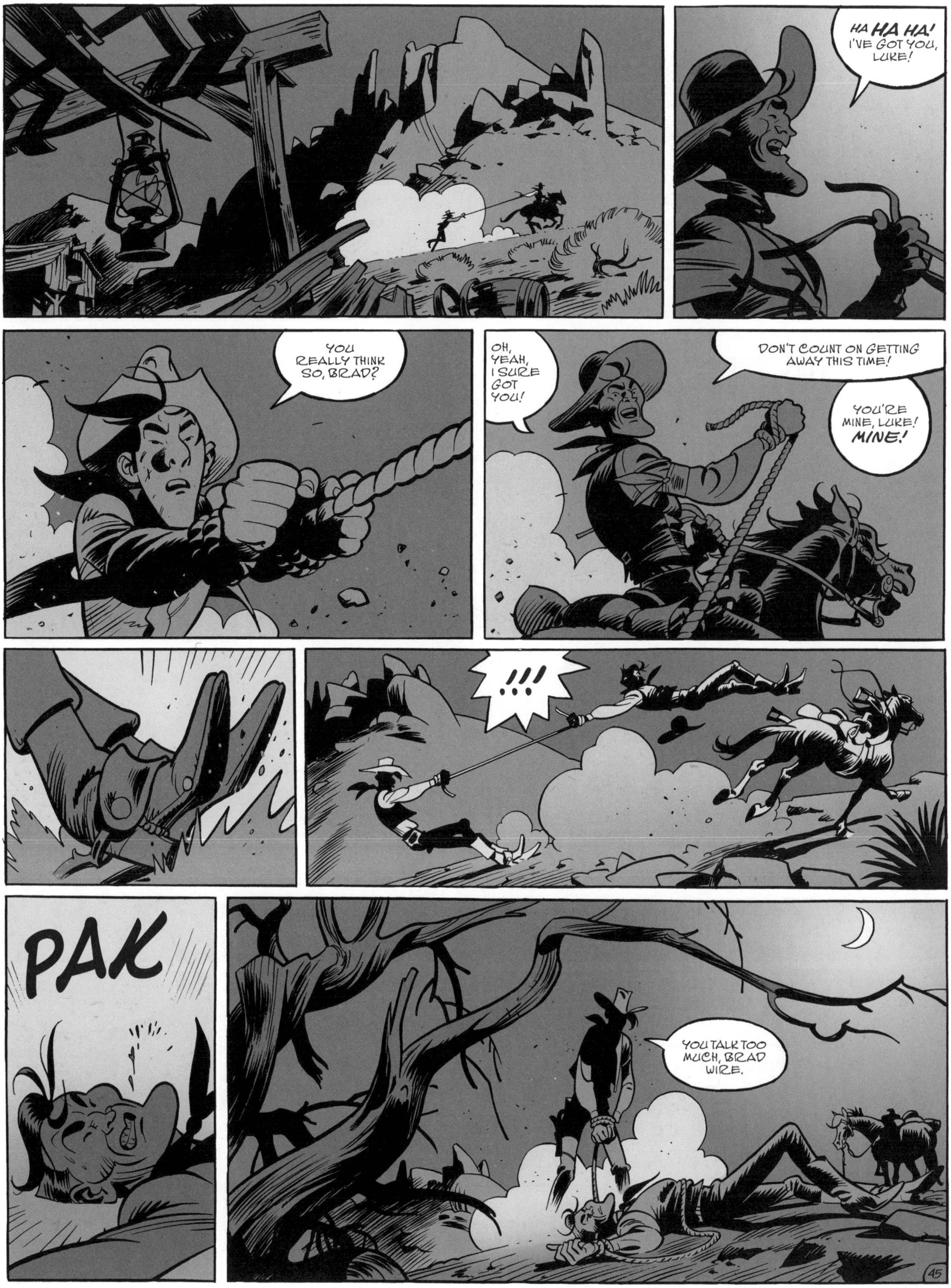

HA HA HA! I'VE GOT YOU, LUKE!
YOU REALLY THINK SO, BRAD?
OH, YEAH, I SURE GOT YOU!
DON'T COUNT ON GETTING AWAY THIS TIME!
YOU'RE MINE, LUKE! MINE!
!!!
PAK
YOU TALK TOO MUCH, BRAD WIRE.
45

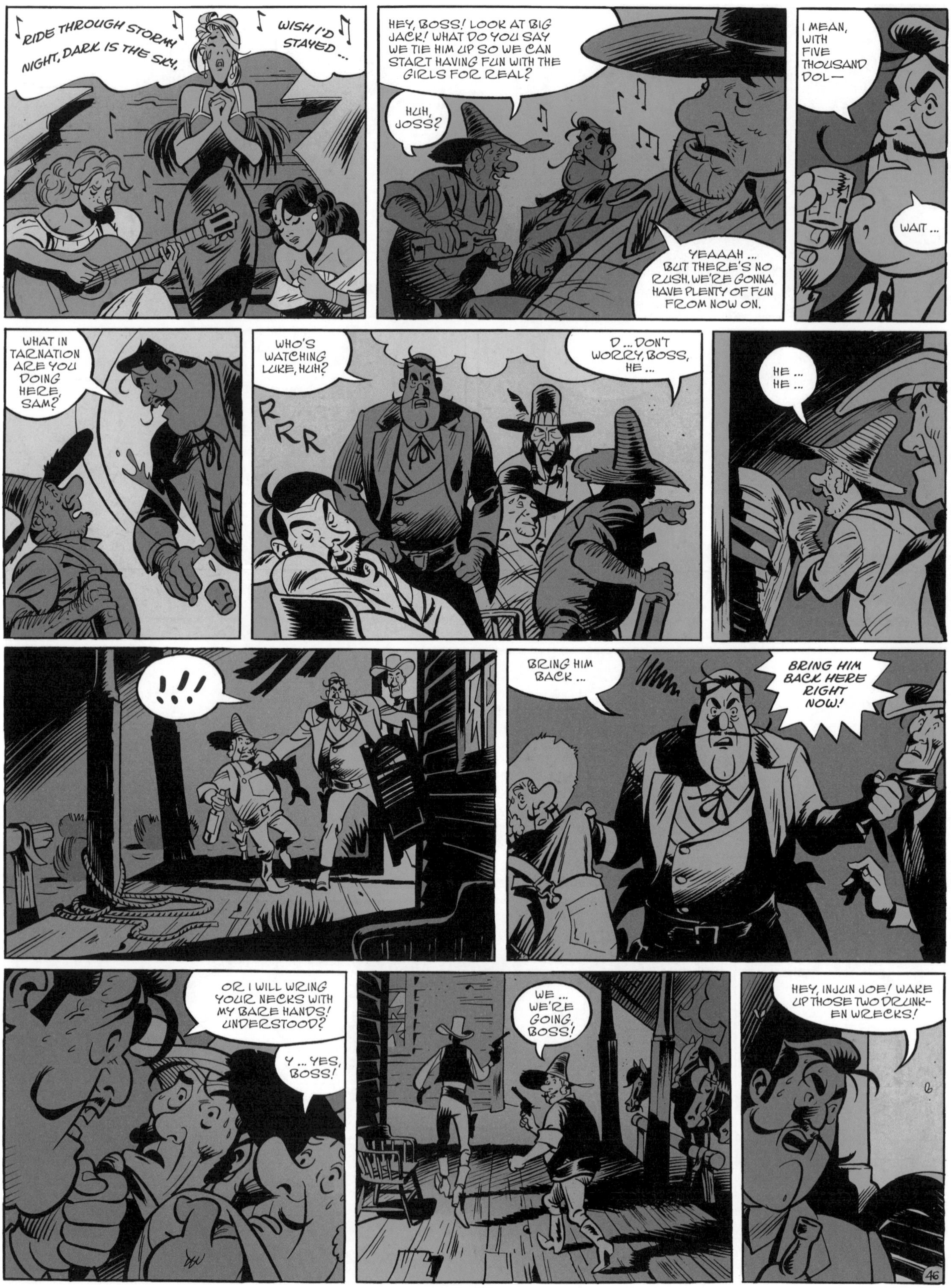
RIDE THROUGH STORMY NIGHT, DARK IS THE SKY,
WISH I'D STAYED ...
HEY, BOSS! LOOK AT BIG JACK! WHAT DO YOU SAY WE TIE HIM UP SO WE CAN START HAVING FUN WITH THE GIRLS FOR REAL?
HUH, JOSS?
YEAAAH ... BUT THERE'S NO RUSH. WE'RE GONNA HAVE PLENTY OF FUN FROM NOW ON.
I MEAN, WITH FIVE THOUSAND DOL—
WAIT ...
WHAT IN TARNATION ARE YOU DOING HERE, SAM?
WHO'S WATCHING LUKE, HUH?
RRR
D ... DON'T WORRY, BOSS, HE ...
HE ... HE ...
!!!
BRING HIM BACK ...
BRING HIM BACK HERE RIGHT NOW!
OR I WILL WRING YOUR NECKS WITH MY BARE HANDS! UNDERSTOOD?
Y ... YES, BOSS!
WE ... WE'RE GOING, BOSS!
HEY, INJUN JOE! WAKE UP THOSE TWO DRUNK-EN WRECKS!
46

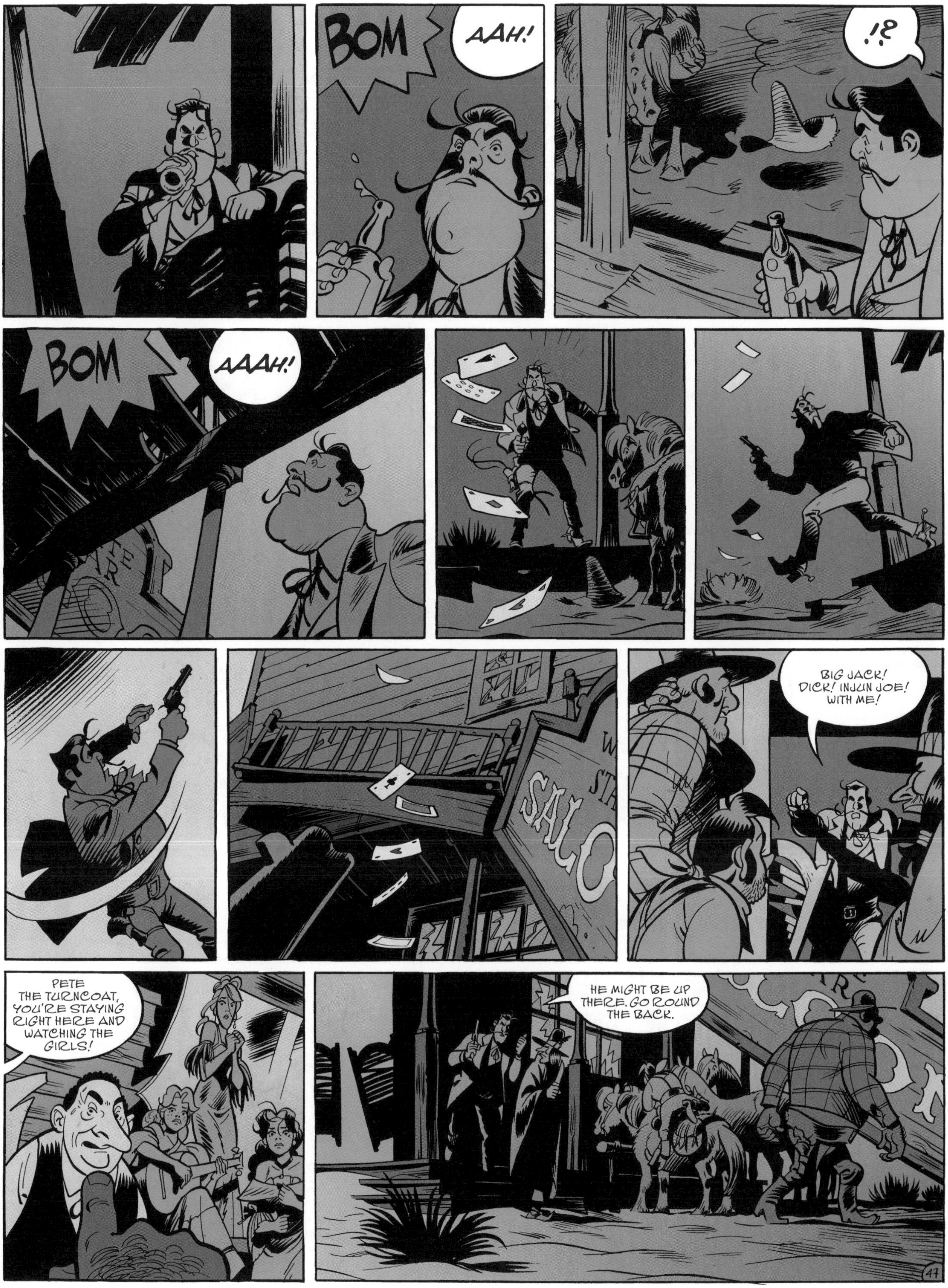
BOM
AAH!
!?
BOM
AAAH!
BIG JACK! DICK! INJUN JOE! WITH ME!
SALO
PETE THE TURNCOAT, YOU'RE STAYING RIGHT HERE AND WATCHING THE GIRLS!
HE MIGHT BE UP THERE. GO ROUND THE BACK.
47

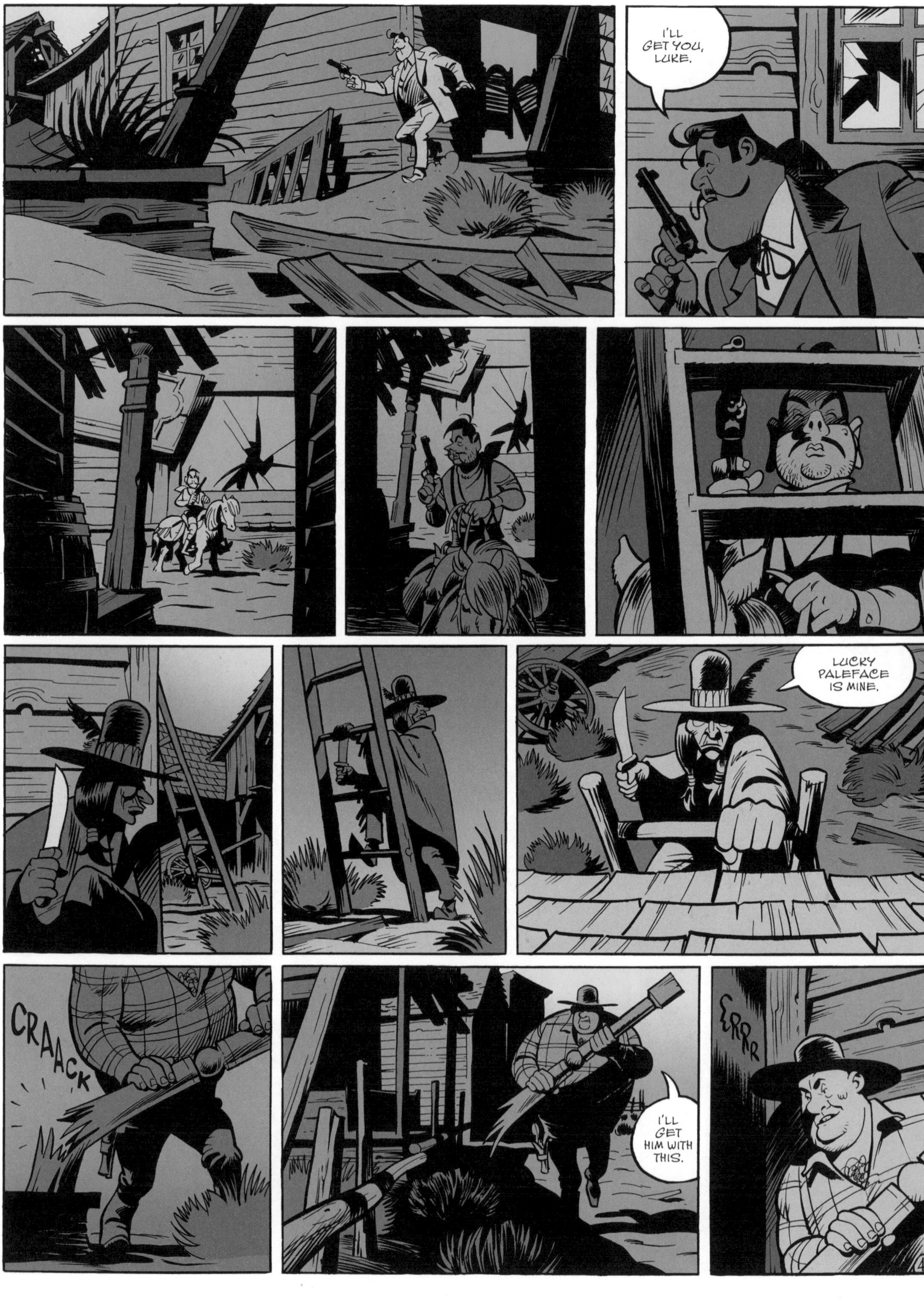
I'LL GET YOU, LUKE.
LUCKY PALEFACE IS MINE.
CRAAACK
I'LL GET HIM WITH THIS.
ERRRR
48

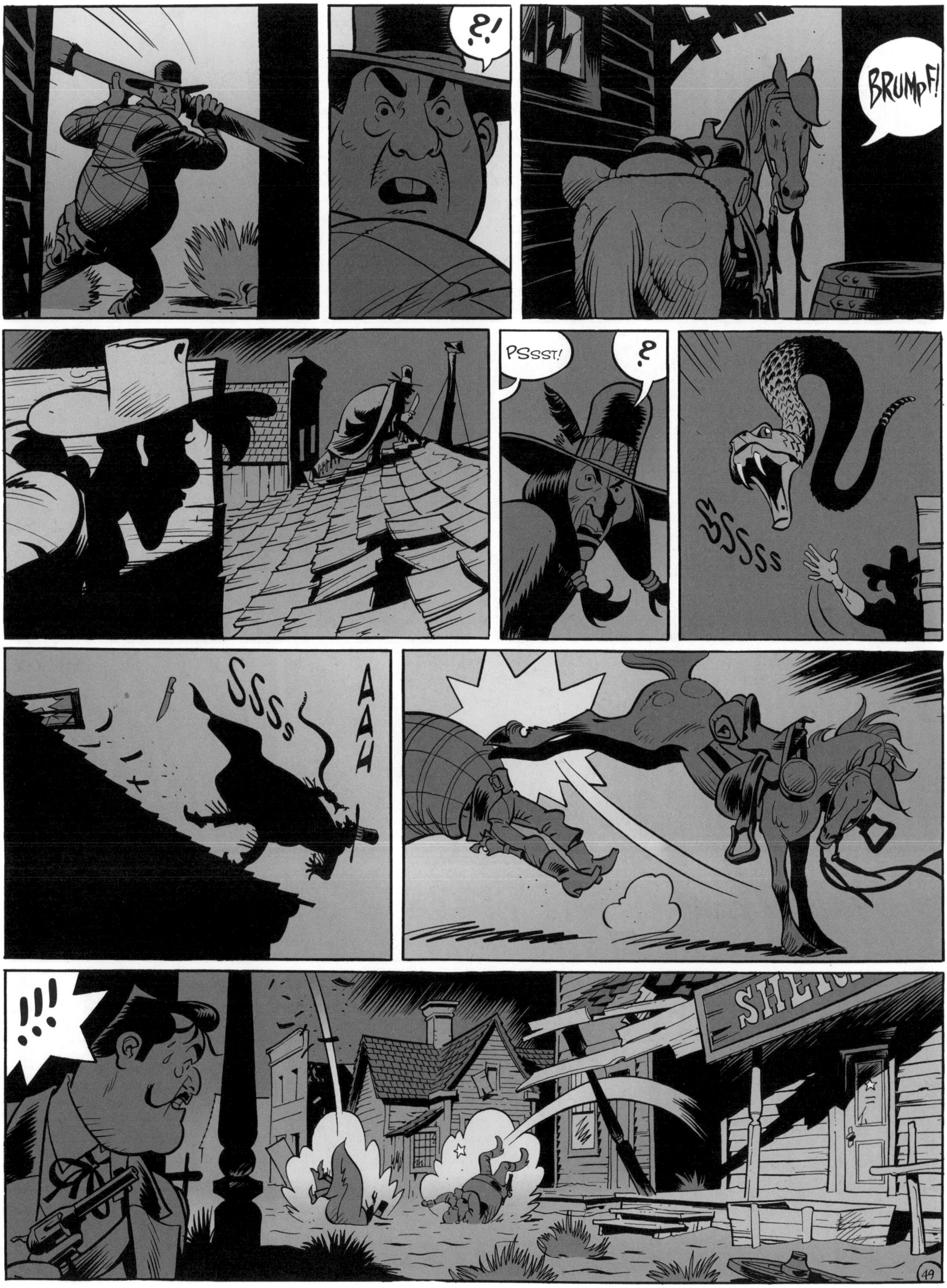
?!
BRUMPF!
PSSST!
?
SSSSS
SSSS
AAH
!!!
SHERIF
49

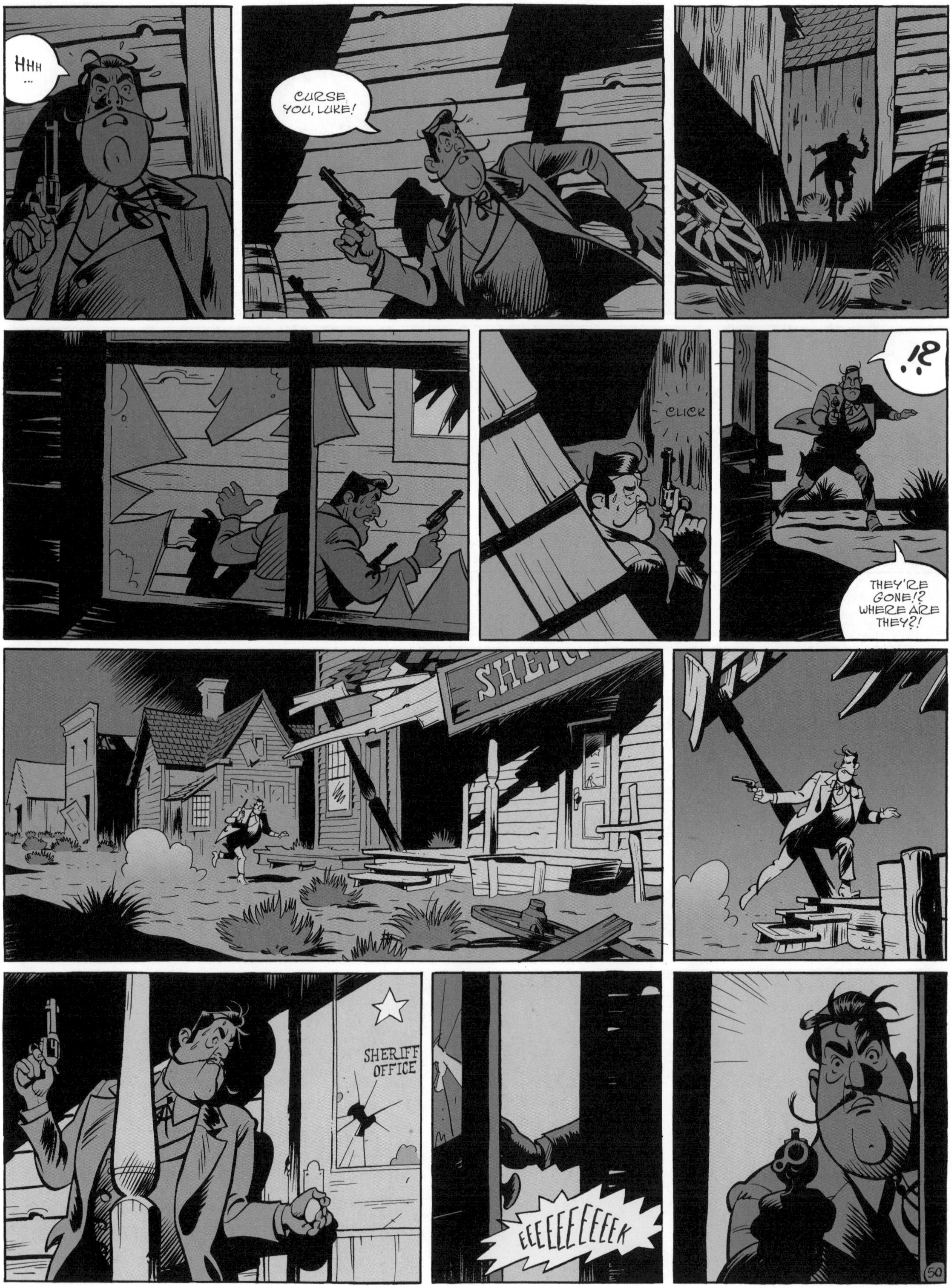
HHH ...
CURSE YOU, LUKE!
CLICK
!?
THEY'RE GONE!? WHERE ARE THEY?!
SHERIFF OFFICE
EEEEEEEEEEK
50

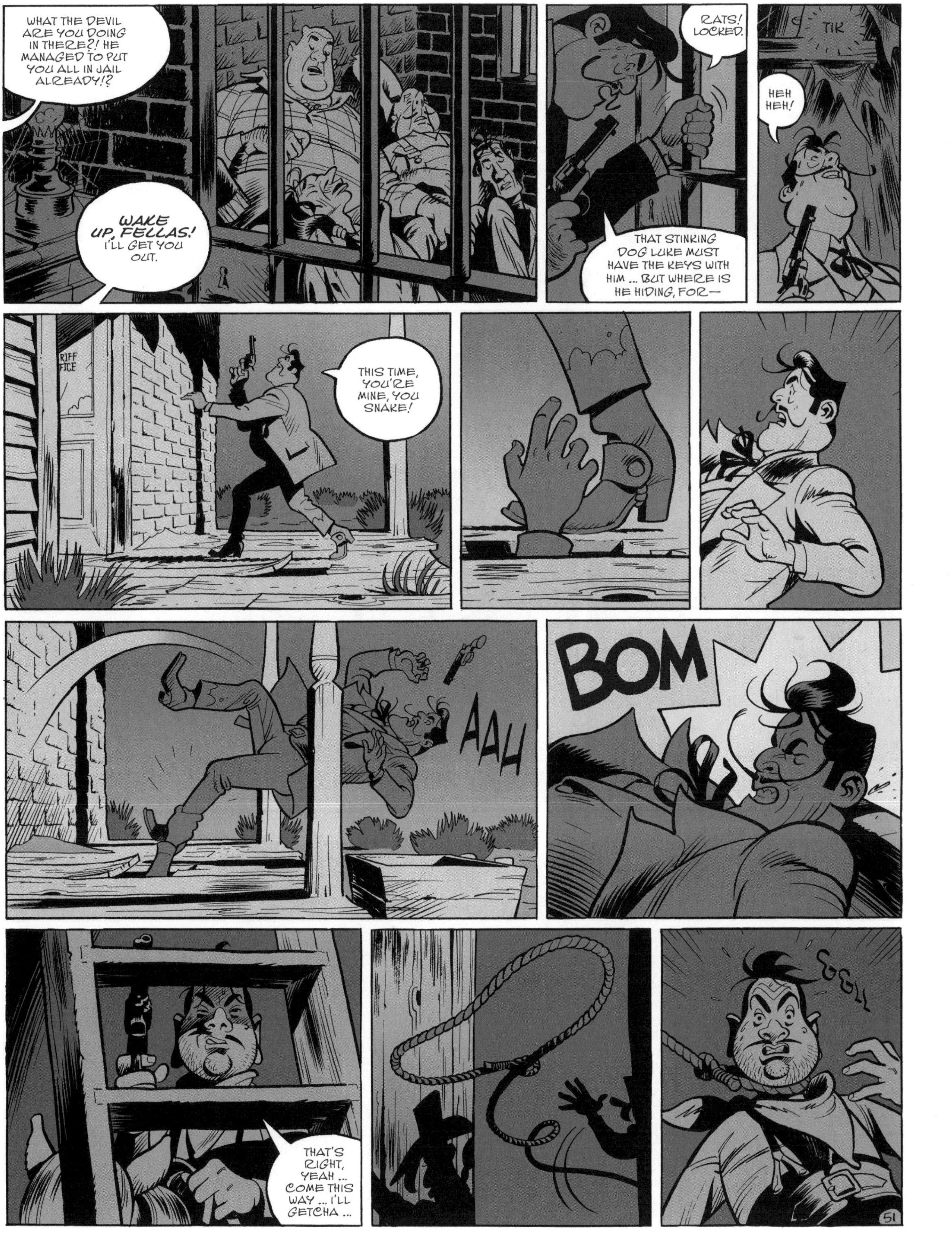
WHAT THE DEVIL ARE YOU DOING IN THERE?! HE MANAGED TO PUT YOU ALL IN JAIL ALREADY!?
WAKE UP, FELLAS! I'LL GET YOU OUT.
RATS! LOCKED.
THAT STINKING DOG LUKE MUST HAVE THE KEYS WITH HIM ... BUT WHERE IS HE HIDING, FOR—
TIK
HEH HEH!
THIS TIME, YOU'RE MINE, YOU SNAKE!
AAH
BOM
THAT'S RIGHT, YEAH ... COME THIS WAY ... I'LL GETCHA ...
51

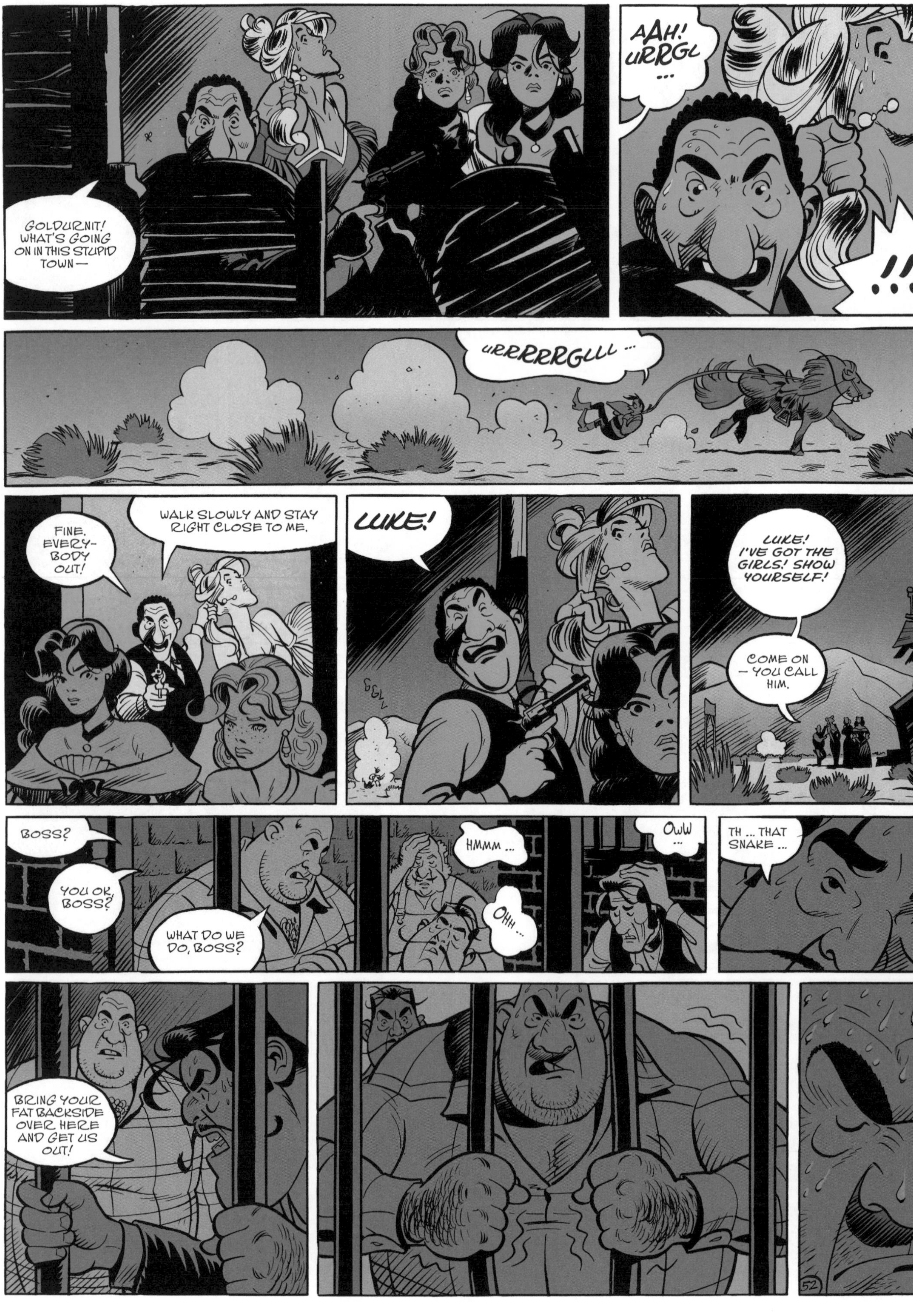
GOLDURNIT! WHAT'S GOING ON IN THIS STUPID TOWN —
AAH! URRGL ...
!!!
URRRRRGLLL ...
FINE. EVERY-BODY OUT!
WALK SLOWLY AND STAY RIGHT CLOSE TO ME.
LUKE!
LUKE! I'VE GOT THE GIRLS! SHOW YOURSELF!
COME ON — YOU CALL HIM.
BOSS?
YOU OK, BOSS?
WHAT DO WE DO, BOSS?
HMMM ...
OHH ...
OWW ...
TH ... THAT SNAKE ...
BRING YOUR FAT BACKSIDE OVER HERE AND GET US OUT!

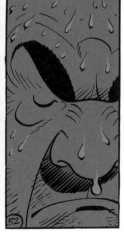

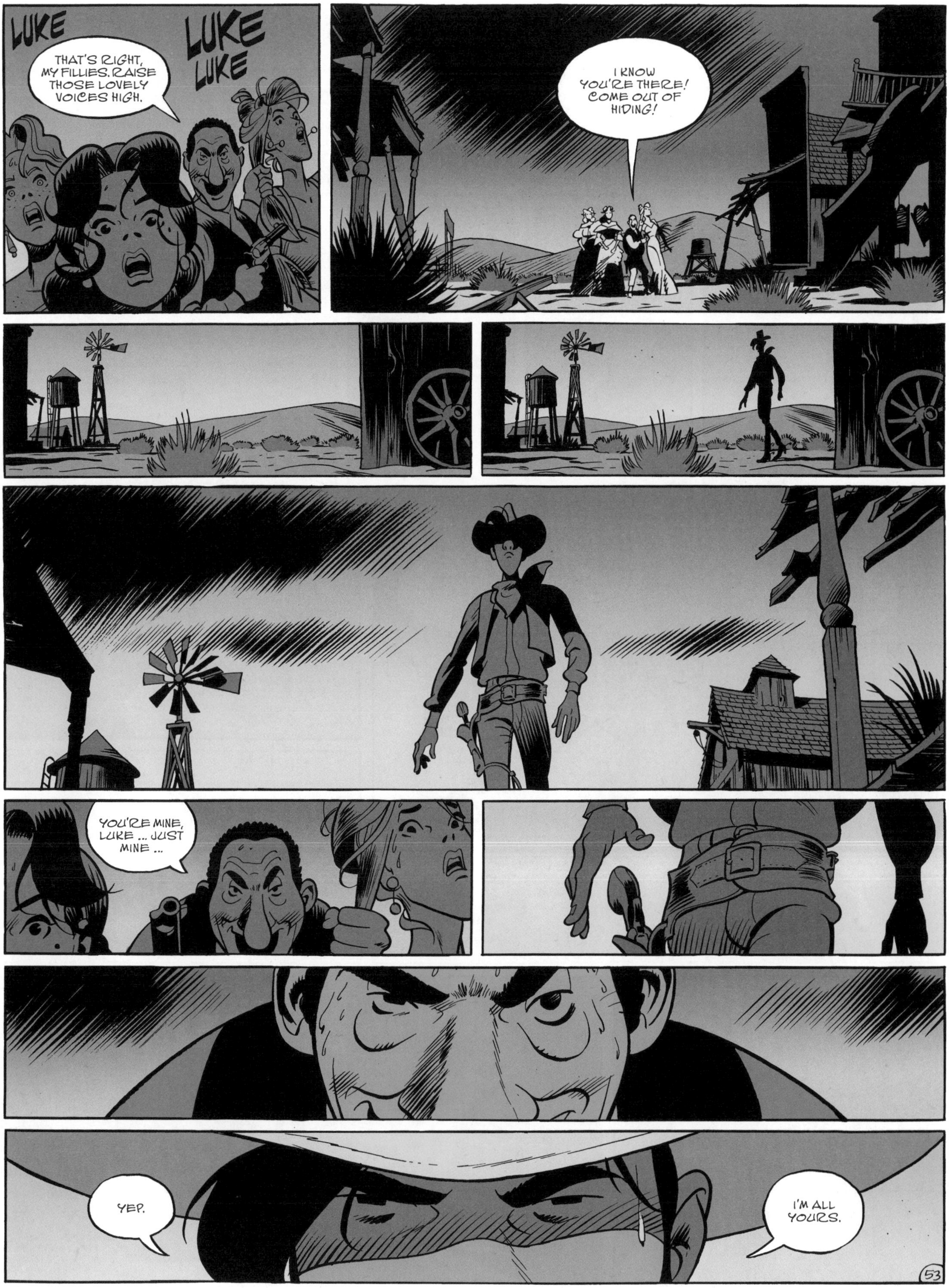
LUKE
LUKE
LUKE
THAT'S RIGHT, MY FILLIES. RAISE THOSE LOVELY VOICES HIGH.
I KNOW YOU'RE THERE! COME OUT OF HIDING!
YOU'RE MINE, LUKE ... JUST MINE ...
YEP.
I'M ALL YOURS.
53

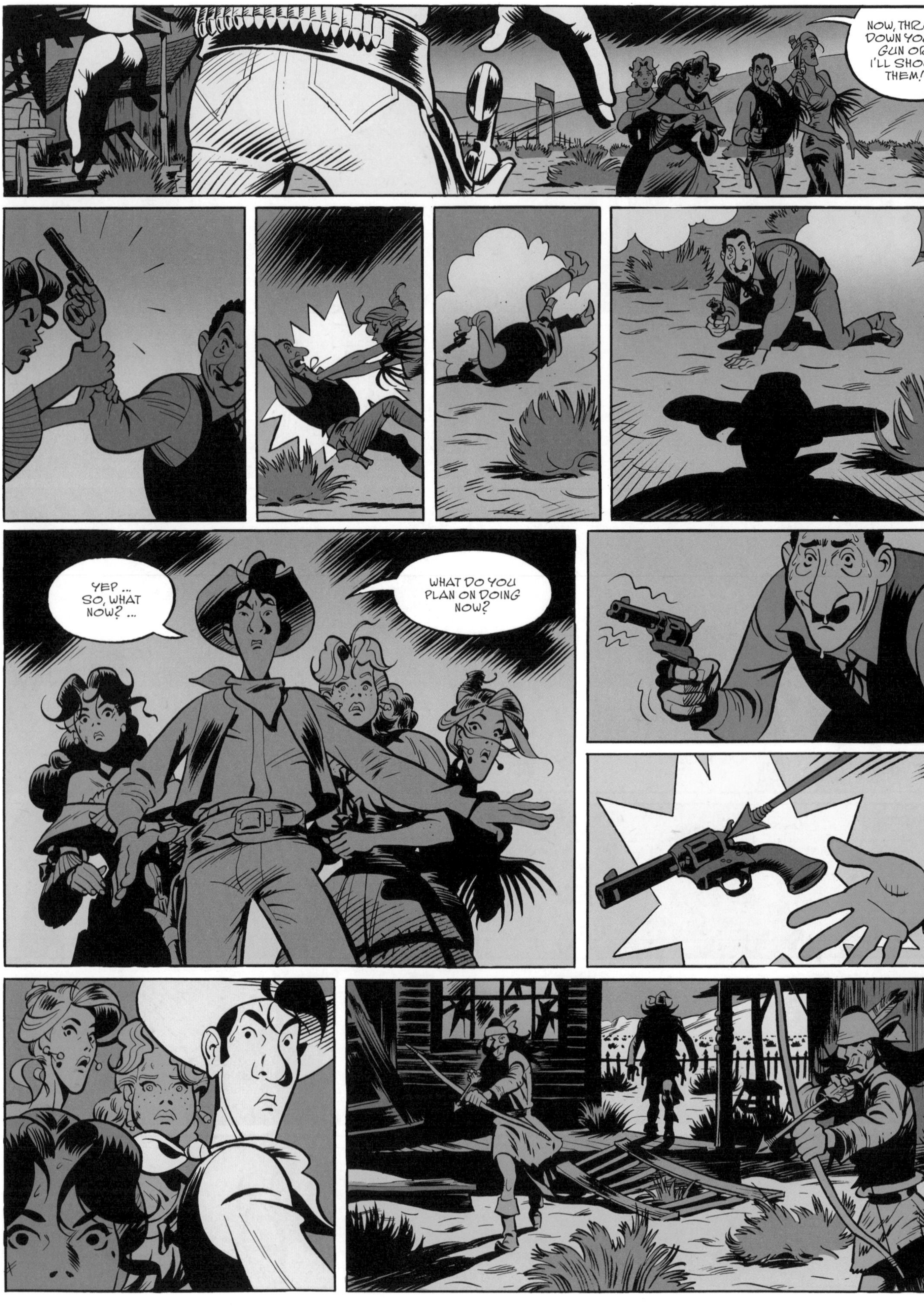
NOW, THROW DOWN YOUR GUN OR I'LL SHOOT THEM!
YEP ... SO, WHAT NOW? ...
WHAT DO YOU PLAN ON DOING NOW?
54

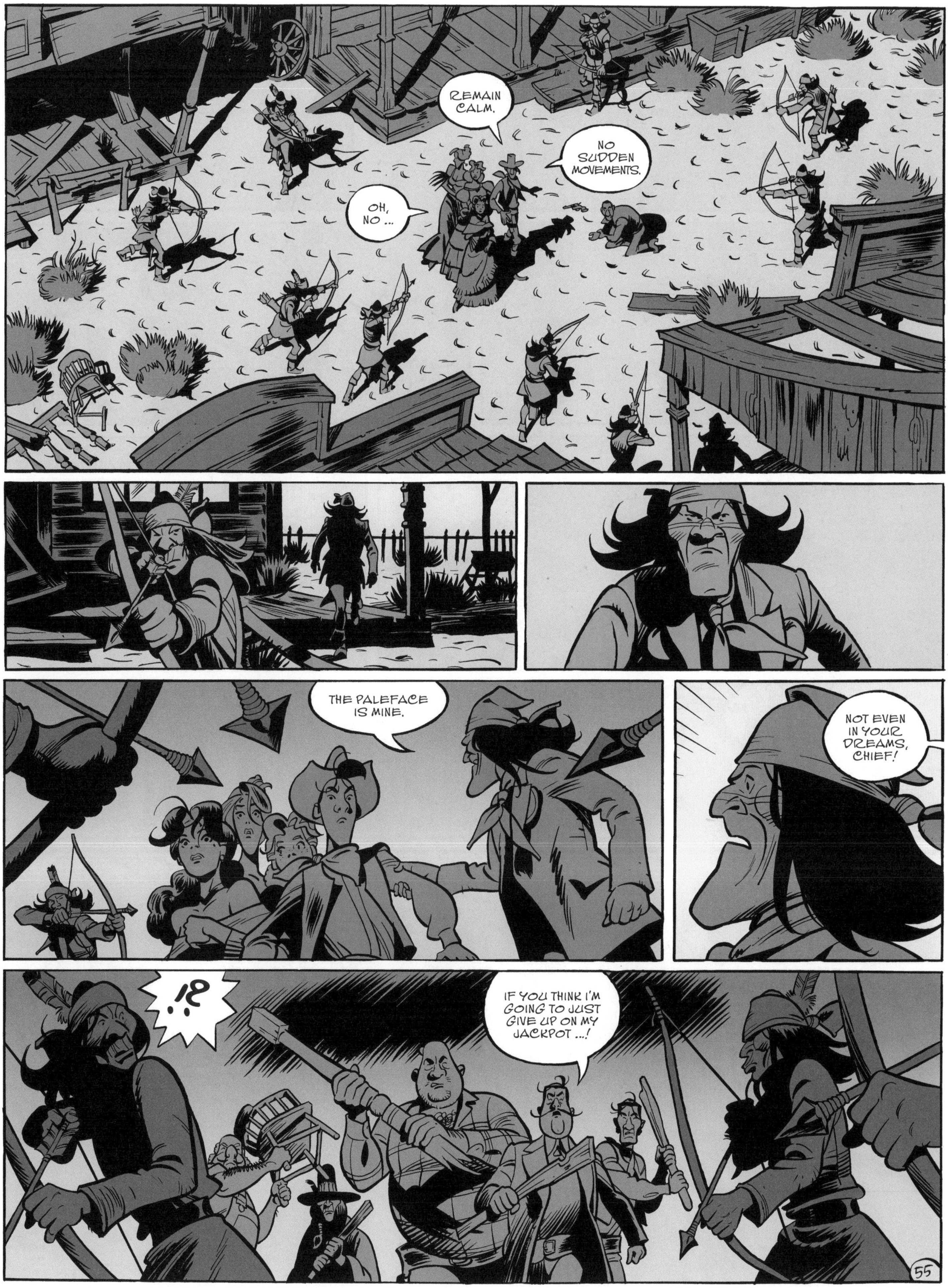
REMAIN CALM.
NO SUDDEN MOVEMENTS.
OH, NO ...
THE PALEFACE IS MINE.
NOT EVEN IN YOUR DREAMS, CHIEF!
!?
IF YOU THINK I'M GOING TO JUST GIVE UP ON MY JACKPOT ...!
55

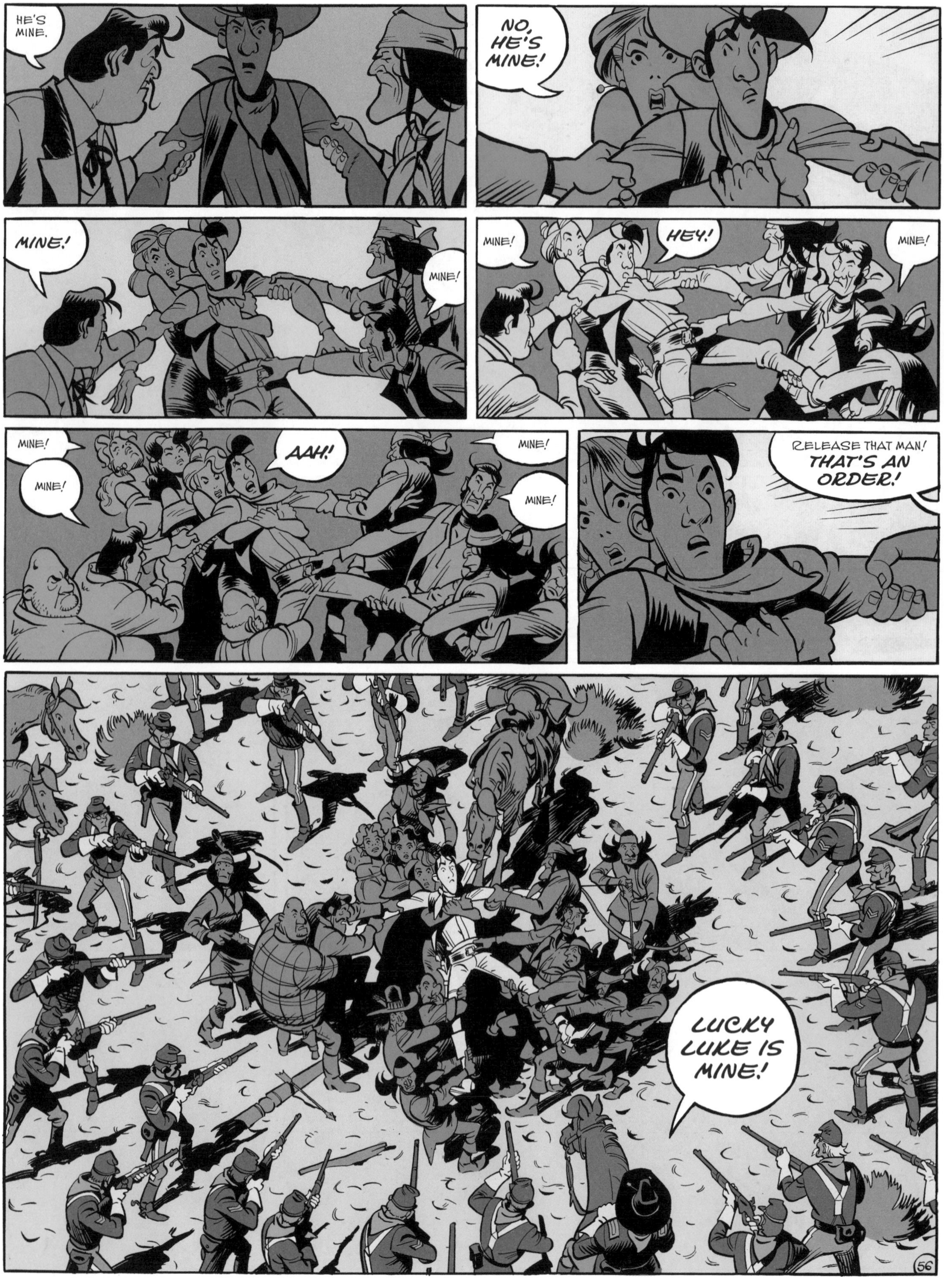
HE'S MINE.
NO, HE'S MINE!
MINE!
MINE!
MINE!
HEY!
MINE!
MINE!
MINE!
AAH!
MINE!
MINE!
RELEASE THAT MAN! THAT'S AN ORDER!
LUCKY LUKE IS MINE!
56

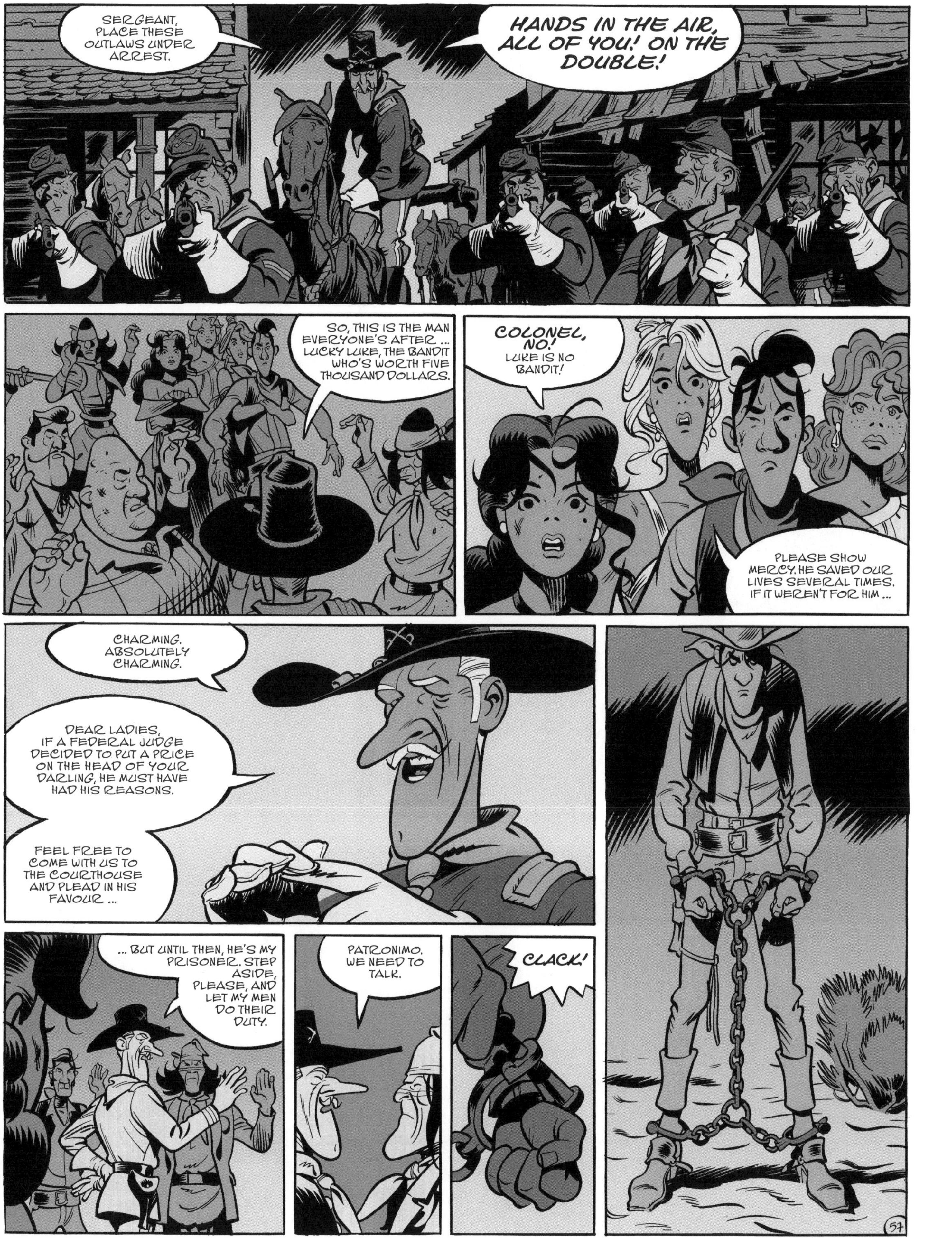
SERGEANT, PLACE THESE OUTLAWS UNDER ARREST.
HANDS IN THE AIR, ALL OF YOU! ON THE DOUBLE!
SO, THIS IS THE MAN EVERYONE'S AFTER ... LUCKY LUKE, THE BANDIT WHO'S WORTH FIVE THOUSAND DOLLARS.
COLONEL, NO! LUKE IS NO BANDIT!
PLEASE SHOW MERCY. HE SAVED OUR LIVES SEVERAL TIMES. IF IT WEREN'T FOR HIM ...
CHARMING. ABSOLUTELY CHARMING.
DEAR LADIES, IF A FEDERAL JUDGE DECIDED TO PUT A PRICE ON THE HEAD OF YOUR DARLING, HE MUST HAVE HAD HIS REASONS.
FEEL FREE TO COME WITH US TO THE COURTHOUSE AND PLEAD IN HIS FAVOUR ...
... BUT UNTIL THEN, HE'S MY PRISONER. STEP ASIDE, PLEASE, AND LET MY MEN DO THEIR DUTY.
PATRONIMO. WE NEED TO TALK.
CLACK!
57

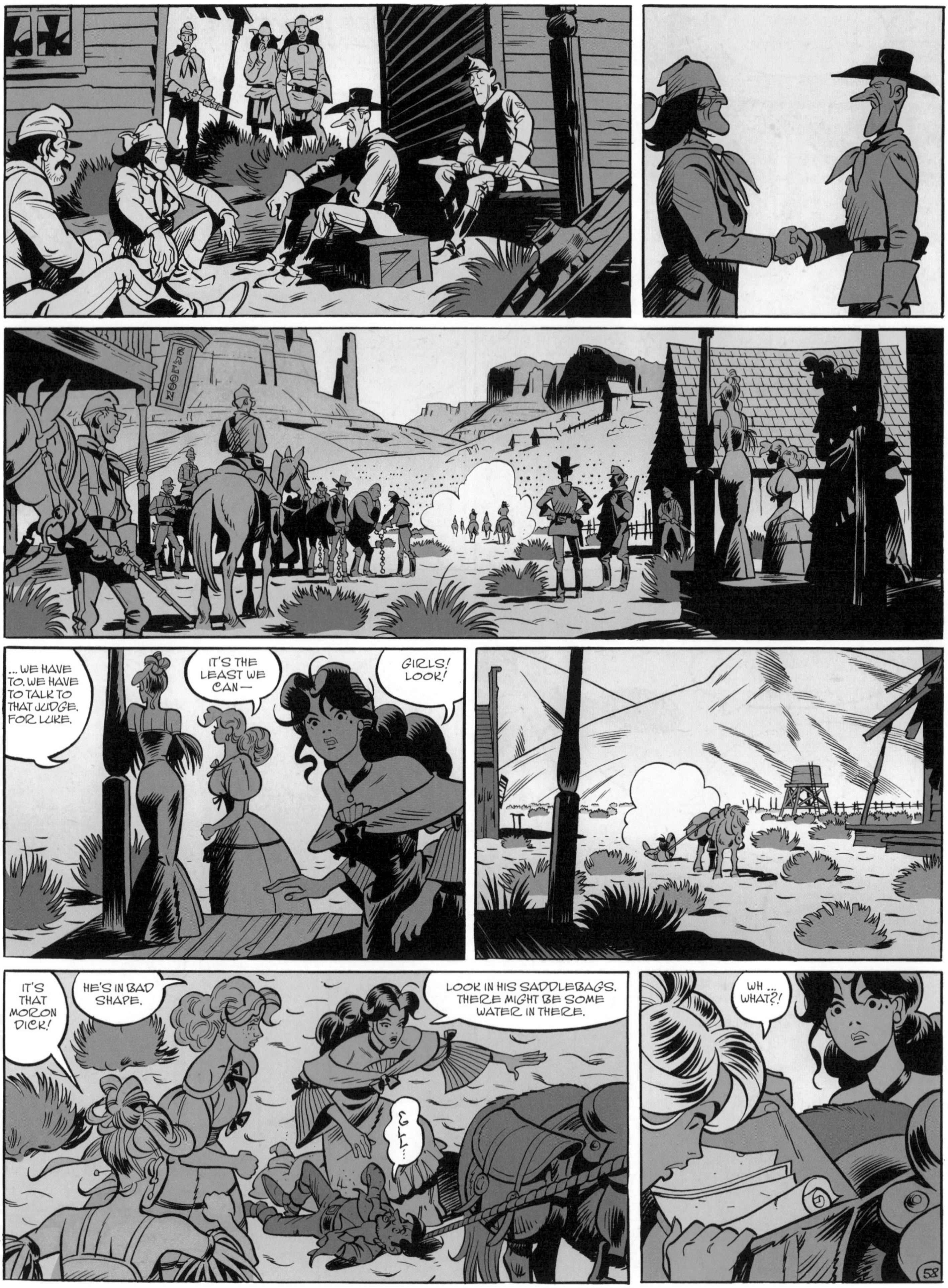
... WE HAVE TO. WE HAVE TO TALK TO THAT JUDGE. FOR LUKE.
IT'S THE LEAST WE CAN—
GIRLS! LOOK!
IT'S THAT MORON DICK!
HE'S IN BAD SHAPE.
LOOK IN HIS SADDLEBAGS. THERE MIGHT BE SOME WATER IN THERE.
ELL...
WH ... WHAT?!
58

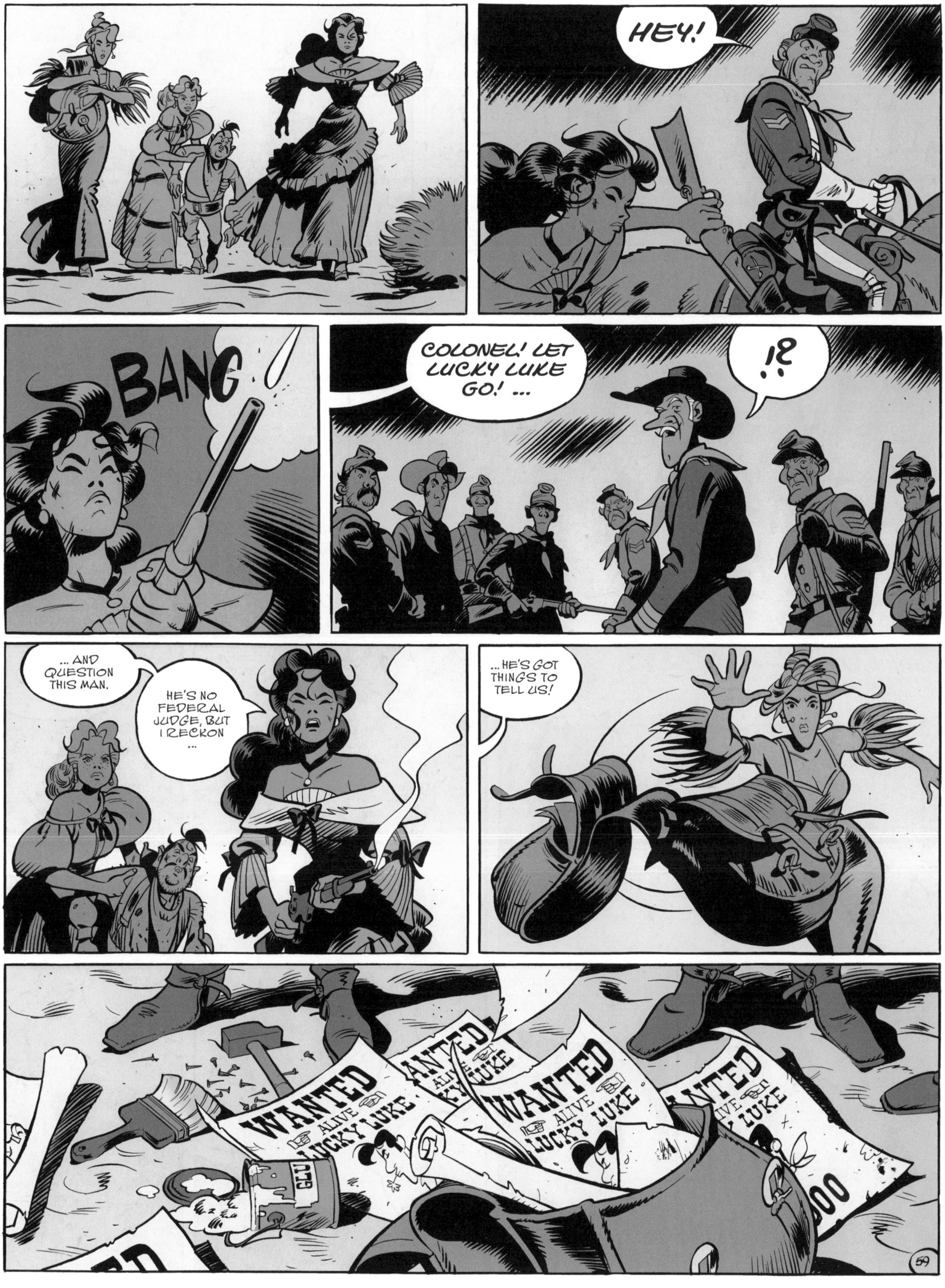
HEY!
BANG
COLONEL! LET LUCKY LUKE GO! ...
!?
... AND QUESTION THIS MAN.
HE'S NO FEDERAL JUDGE, BUT I RECKON ...
... HE'S GOT THINGS TO TELL US!
WANTED
ALIVE
LUCKY LUKE
WANTED
ALIVE
LUCKY LUKE
59

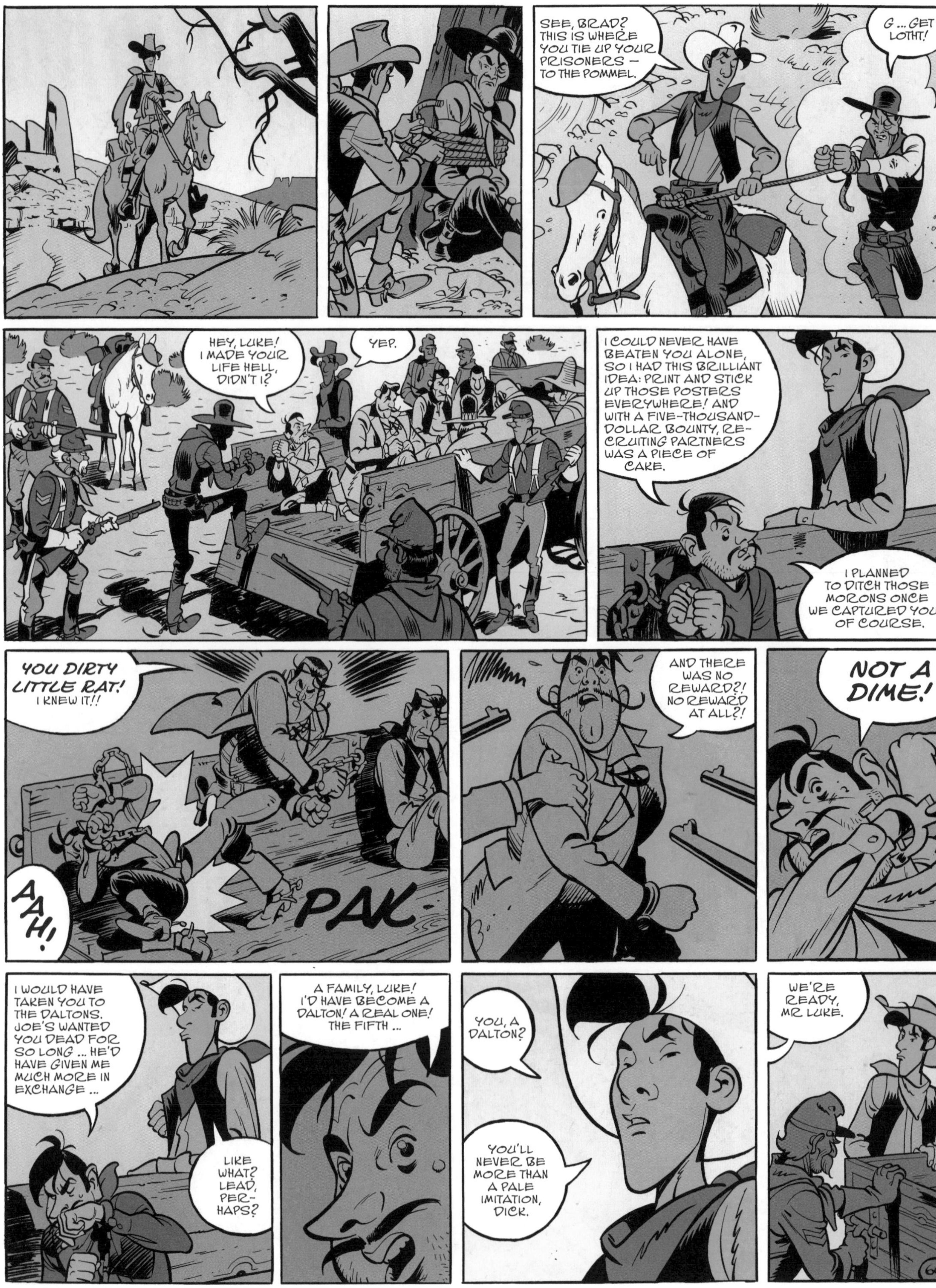

SEE, BRAD? THIS IS WHERE YOU TIE UP YOUR PRISONERS — TO THE POMMEL.
G ... GET LOTHT!
HEY, LUKE! I MADE YOUR LIFE HELL, DIDN'T I?
YEP.
I COULD NEVER HAVE BEATEN YOU ALONE, SO I HAD THIS BRILLIANT IDEA: PRINT AND STICK UP THOSE POSTERS EVERYWHERE! AND WITH A FIVE-THOUSAND-DOLLAR BOUNTY, RECRUITING PARTNERS WAS A PIECE OF CAKE.
I PLANNED TO DITCH THOSE MORONS ONCE WE CAPTURED YOU, OF COURSE.
YOU DIRTY LITTLE RAT! I KNEW IT!!
AAH!
PAK
AND THERE WAS NO REWARD?! NO REWARD AT ALL?!
NOT A DIME!
I WOULD HAVE TAKEN YOU TO THE DALTONS. JOE'S WANTED YOU DEAD FOR SO LONG ... HE'D HAVE GIVEN ME MUCH MORE IN EXCHANGE ...
LIKE WHAT? LEAD, PERHAPS?
A FAMILY, LUKE! I'D HAVE BECOME A DALTON! A REAL ONE! THE FIFTH ...
YOU, A DALTON?
YOU'LL NEVER BE MORE THAN A PALE IMITATION, DICK.
WE'RE READY, MR LUKE.
60

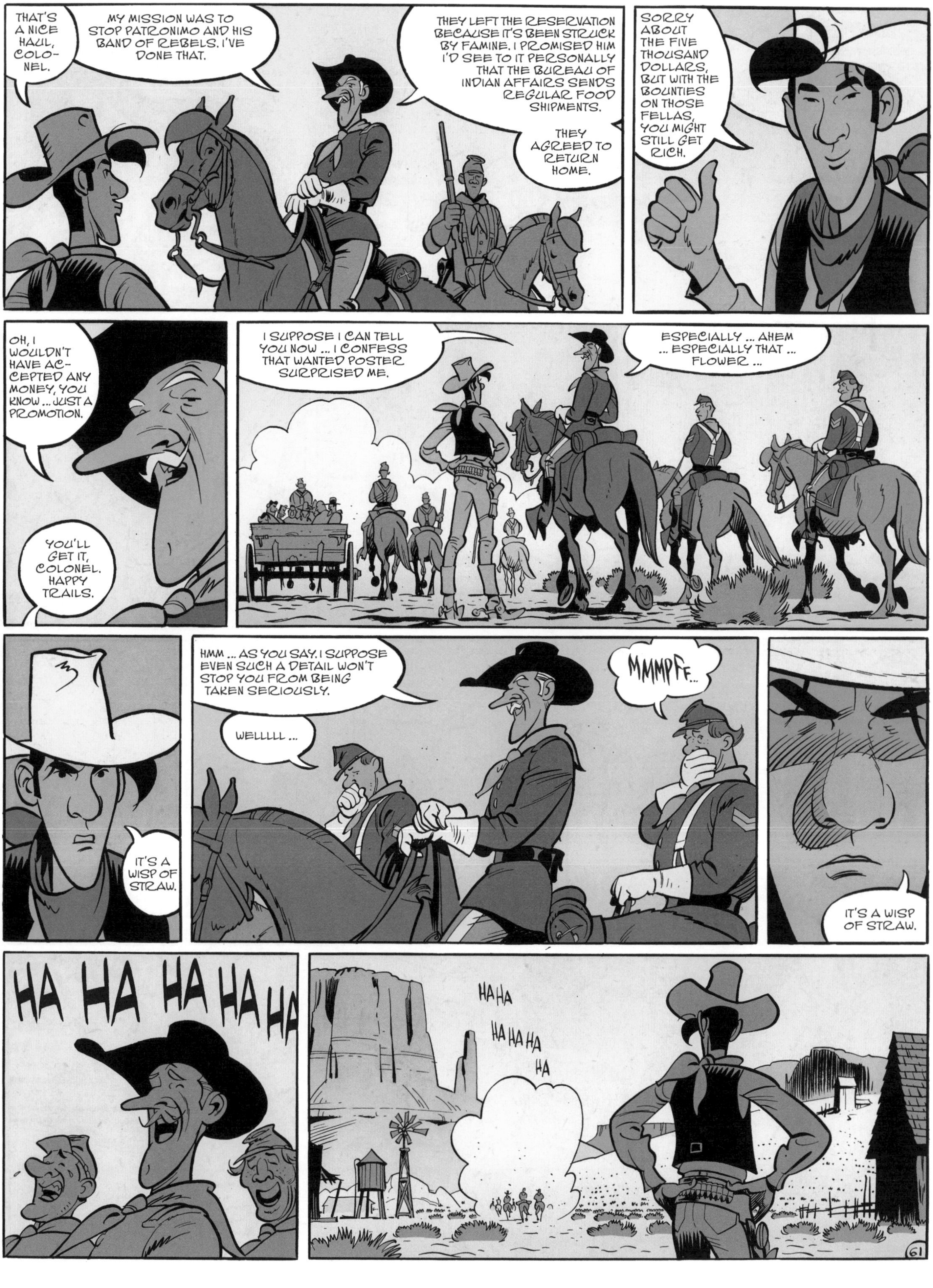
THAT'S A NICE HAUL, COLO- NEL.
MY MISSION WAS TO STOP PATRONIMO AND HIS BAND OF REBELS. I'VE DONE THAT.
THEY LEFT THE RESERVATION BECAUSE IT'S BEEN STRUCK BY FAMINE. I PROMISED HIM I'D SEE TO IT PERSONALLY THAT THE BUREAU OF INDIAN AFFAIRS SENDS REGULAR FOOD SHIPMENTS.
THEY AGREED TO RETURN HOME.
SORRY ABOUT THE FIVE THOUSAND DOLLARS, BUT WITH THE BOUNTIES ON THOSE FELLAS, YOU MIGHT STILL GET RICH.
OH, I WOULDN'T HAVE AC- CEPTED ANY MONEY, YOU KNOW ... JUST A PROMOTION.
YOU'LL GET IT, COLONEL. HAPPY TRAILS.
I SUPPOSE I CAN TELL YOU NOW ... I CONFESS THAT WANTED POSTER SURPRISED ME.
ESPECIALLY ... AHEM ... ESPECIALLY THAT ... FLOWER ...
IT'S A WISP OF STRAW.
HMM ... AS YOU SAY. I SUPPOSE EVEN SUCH A DETAIL WON'T STOP YOU FROM BEING TAKEN SERIOUSLY.
WELLLLL ...
MMMPFF...
IT'S A WISP OF STRAW.
HA HA HA HA HA
HA HA
HA HA HA
HA
61

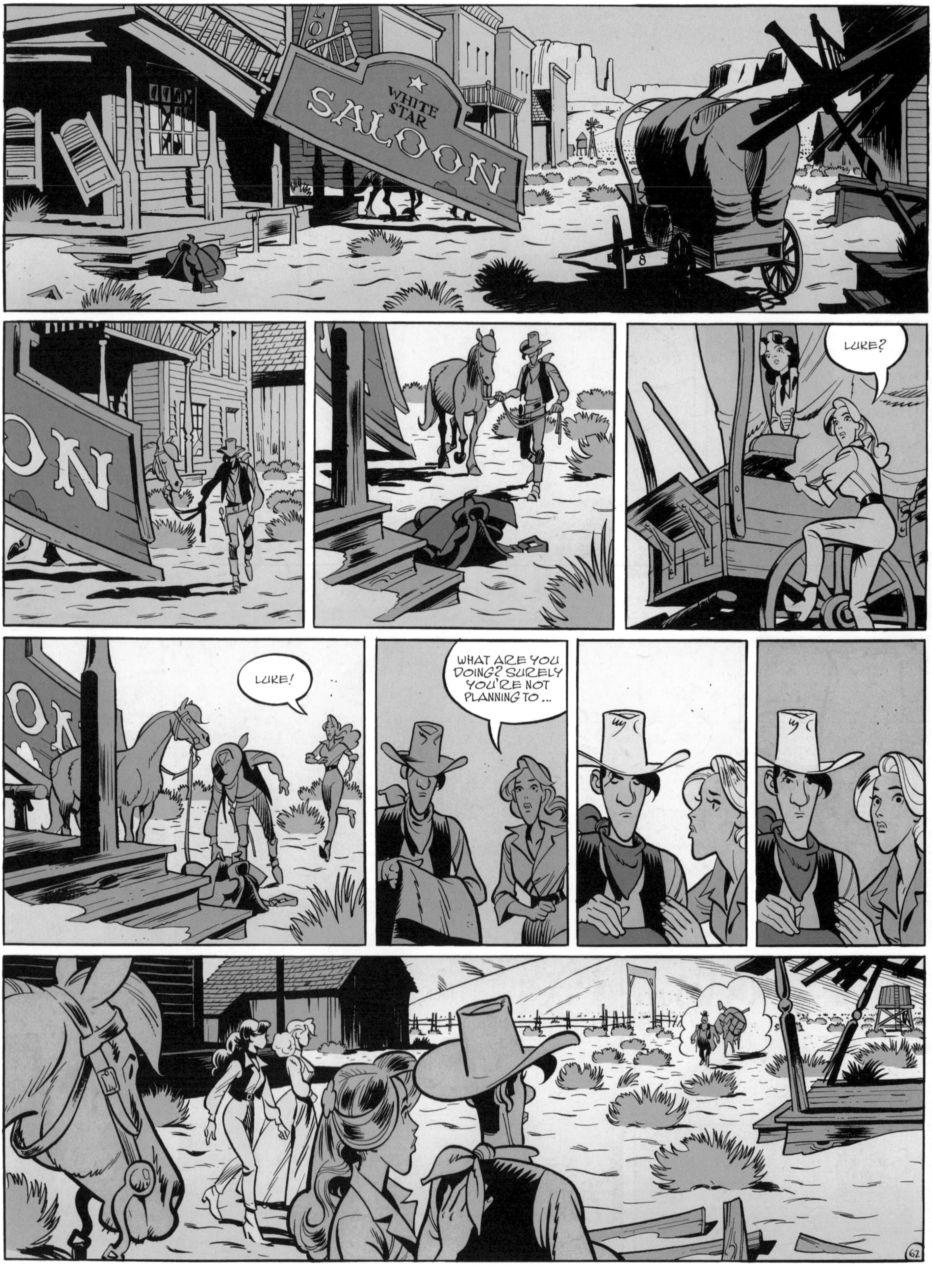
WHITE STAR
SALOON
LUKE?
LUKE!
WHAT ARE YOU DOING? SURELY YOU'RE NOT PLANNING TO ...
62

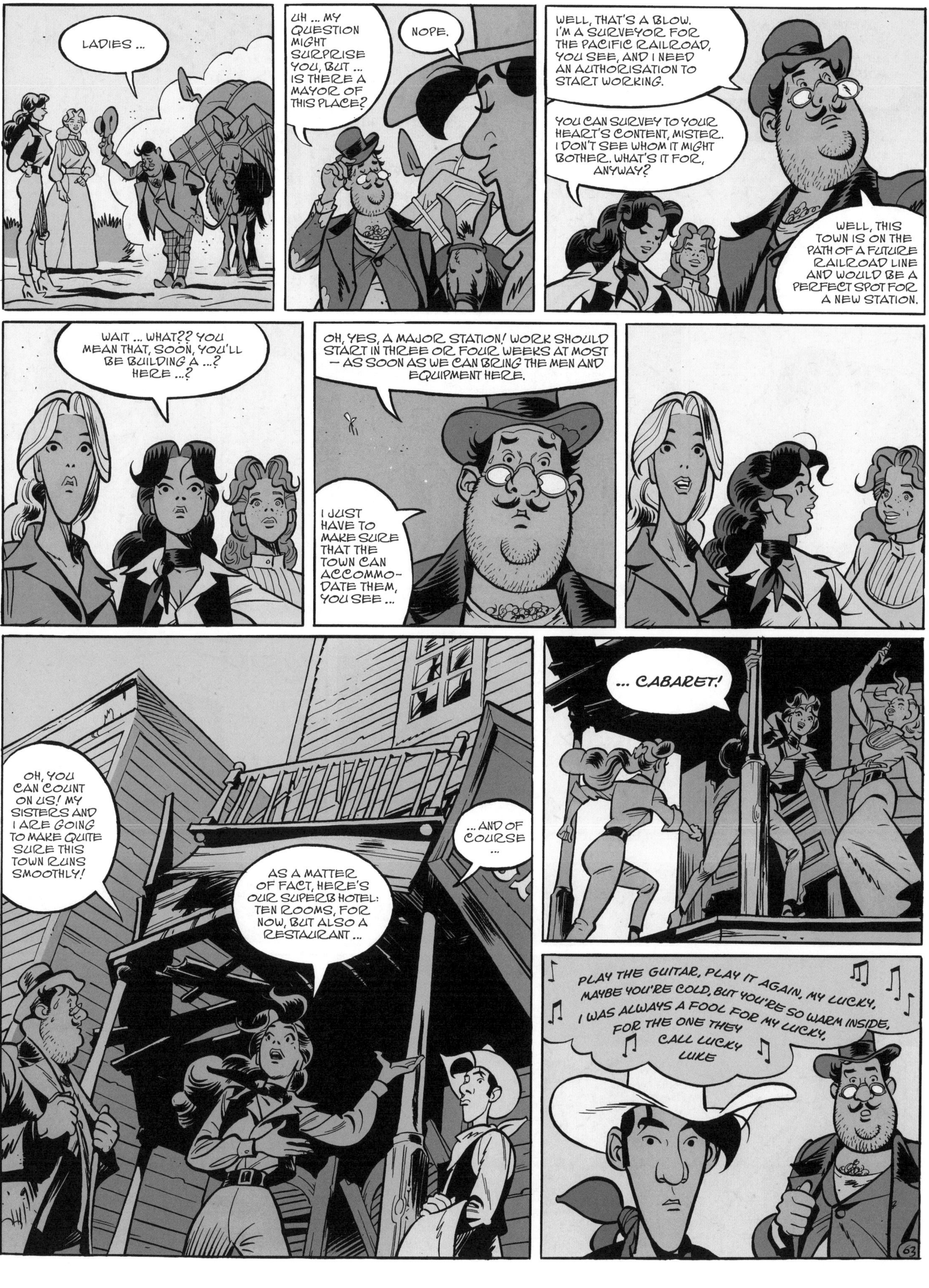
LADIES ...
UH ... MY QUESTION MIGHT SURPRISE YOU, BUT ... IS THERE A MAYOR OF THIS PLACE?
NOPE.
WELL, THAT'S A BLOW. I'M A SURVEYOR FOR THE PACIFIC RAILROAD, YOU SEE, AND I NEED AN AUTHORISATION TO START WORKING.
YOU CAN SURVEY TO YOUR HEART'S CONTENT, MISTER. I DON'T SEE WHOM IT MIGHT BOTHER. WHAT'S IT FOR, ANYWAY?
WELL, THIS TOWN IS ON THE PATH OF A FUTURE RAILROAD LINE AND WOULD BE A PERFECT SPOT FOR A NEW STATION.
WAIT ... WHAT?? YOU MEAN THAT, SOON, YOU'LL BE BUILDING A ...? HERE ...?
OH, YES, A MAJOR STATION! WORK SHOULD START IN THREE OR FOUR WEEKS AT MOST – AS SOON AS WE CAN BRING THE MEN AND EQUIPMENT HERE.
I JUST HAVE TO MAKE SURE THAT THE TOWN CAN ACCOMMODATE THEM, YOU SEE ...
OH, YOU CAN COUNT ON US! MY SISTERS AND I ARE GOING TO MAKE QUITE SURE THIS TOWN RUNS SMOOTHLY!
AS A MATTER OF FACT, HERE'S OUR SUPERB HOTEL: TEN ROOMS, FOR NOW, BUT ALSO A RESTAURANT ...
... AND OF COURSE ...
... CABARET!
PLAY THE GUITAR, PLAY IT AGAIN, MY LUCKY,
MAYBE YOU'RE COLD, BUT YOU'RE SO WARM INSIDE,
I WAS ALWAYS A FOOL FOR MY LUCKY,
FOR THE ONE THEY CALL LUCKY LUKE
63

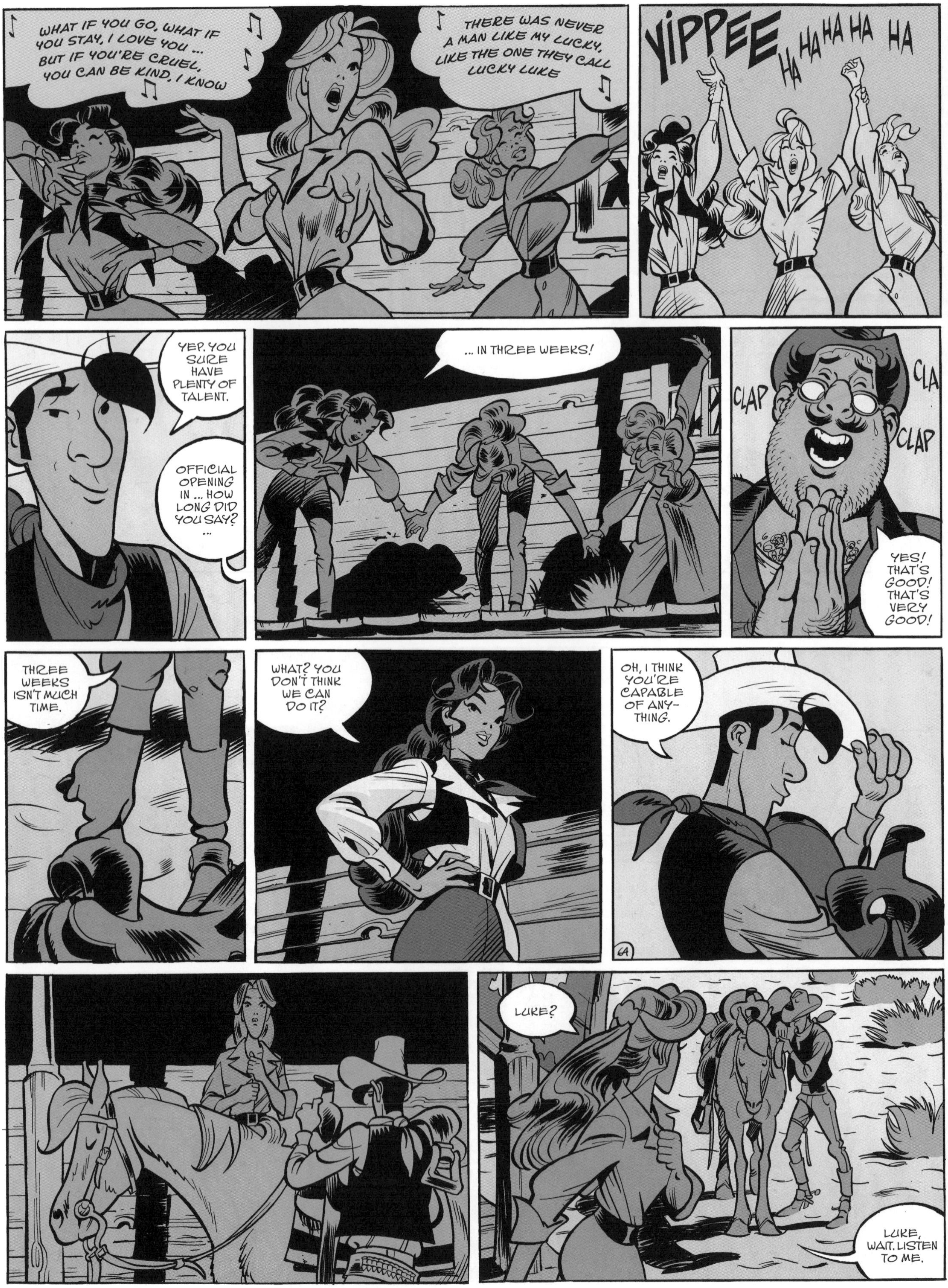
WHAT IF YOU GO, WHAT IF YOU STAY, I LOVE YOU ... BUT IF YOU'RE CRUEL, YOU CAN BE KIND, I KNOW
THERE WAS NEVER A MAN LIKE MY LUCKY, LIKE THE ONE THEY CALL LUCKY LUKE
YIPPEE HA HA HA HA HA
YEP. YOU SURE HAVE PLENTY OF TALENT.
OFFICIAL OPENING IN ... HOW LONG DID YOU SAY? ...
... IN THREE WEEKS!
CLAP CLAP CLAP
YES! THAT'S GOOD! THAT'S VERY GOOD!
THREE WEEKS ISN'T MUCH TIME.
WHAT? YOU DON'T THINK WE CAN DO IT?
OH, I THINK YOU'RE CAPABLE OF ANY-THING.
LUKE?
LUKE, WAIT. LISTEN TO ME.

WHEN I WAS A LITTLE GIRL, ON THE RANCH, I HAD A KITTEN ...

... HE WOULD ALWAYS COME TO ME, BEGGING TO BE PETTED. BUT AS SOON AS I'D REACH OUT FOR HIM, HE'D SCRATCH ME.

ONE DAY WHEN IT MADE ME CRY, MY GRANDMOTHER EXPLAINED THAT HE'D BEEN SEPARATED FROM HIS MOTHER TOO EARLY. SHE SAID, 'WHEN YOU HAVEN'T RECEIVED ANY LOVE, IT'S VERY HARD TO GIVE ANY.'

IT MIGHT SOUND CRAZY TO YOU, BUT ...

... I THINK LOVE IS SOMETHING YOU LEARN.

I ...

I COULD TEACH YOU, LUKE.

CHERRY ...

LUKE, I ... I SO WOULD HAVE LIKED—

I KNOW.

I SO WOULD HAVE TOO ...

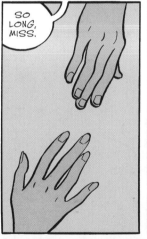

SO LONG, MISS.

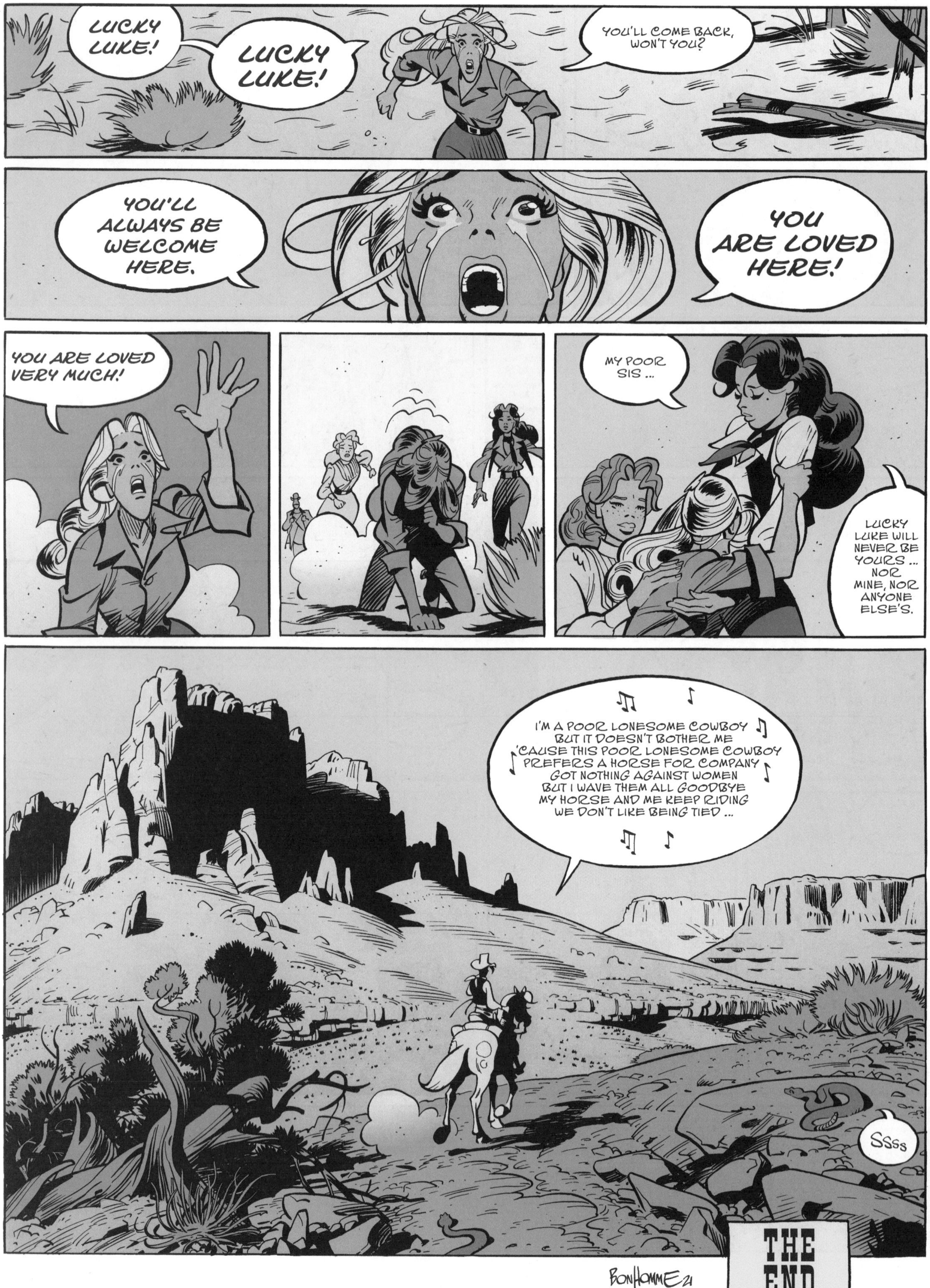

LUCKY LUKE!
LUCKY LUKE!
YOU'LL COME BACK, WON'T YOU?
YOU'LL ALWAYS BE WELCOME HERE.
YOU ARE LOVED HERE!
YOU ARE LOVED VERY MUCH!
MY POOR SIS ...
LUCKY LUKE WILL NEVER BE YOURS ... NOR MINE, NOR ANYONE ELSE'S.
I'M A POOR LONESOME COWBOY BUT IT DOESN'T BOTHER ME 'CAUSE THIS POOR LONESOME COWBOY PREFERS A HORSE FOR COMPANY GOT NOTHING AGAINST WOMEN BUT I WAVE THEM ALL GOODBYE MY HORSE AND ME KEEP RIDING WE DON'T LIKE BEING TIED ...
SSSS
THE END
BONHOMME 21